# HIT AND RUN

The rifle slug tore into the bench where Longarm had sat an instant before. He and the sheriff dove to one side as a second round buzzed past like an angry hornet. Longarm snapped a shot from his six-gun at the smoke peeking over the roof edge across the plaza.

He hissed at the sheriff. "Cover me! I have his position!"

He ran across the square, with pigeons, kids and nurse-maids scattering out of his path as he zigzagged with his smoking gun in his hand. Longarm reached the building and tore four stories up the stairwell. He burst onto the roof, spinning around with his gun ready to face the assassin. He was alone.

The sheriff caught up to him, calling out before he came up so he wouldn't get shot at.

Longarm remarked, "Long gone. I zigged all them zags for nothing. He, she, or it took the shots, and hightailed it down the stairs before I even got across the plaza."

He spat angrily.

"I *hate* it when they do that."

TABOR EVANS

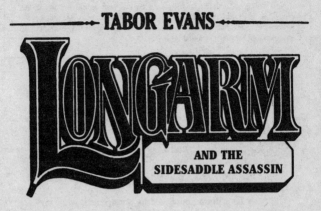

# LONGARM

## AND THE
## SIDESADDLE ASSASSIN

JOVE BOOKS, NEW YORK

## LONGARM AND THE SIDESADDLE ASSASSIN

A Jove Book / published by arrangement with
the author

PRINTING HISTORY
Jove edition / January 2002

All rights reserved.
Copyright © 2002 by Penguin Putnam Inc.
This book, or parts thereof, may not be reproduced in any form
without permission.
For information address: The Berkley Publishing Group,
a division of Penguin Putnam Inc.,
375 Hudson Street, New York, New York 10014.

Visit our website at
www.penguinputnam.com

ISBN: 0-515-13232-2

A JOVE BOOK®
Jove Books are published by The Berkley Publishing Group,
a division of Penguin Putnam Inc.,
375 Hudson Street, New York, New York 10014.
JOVE and the "J" design
are trademarks belonging to Penguin Putnam Inc.

PRINTED IN THE UNITED STATES OF AMERICA

10  9  8  7  6  5  4  3  2  1

# Chapter 1

That priss who'd first said virtue was its own reward had never shown up for work on time with a paid assassin laying for him on a rooftop across the street. It was going on nine A.M. Even the high-and-mighty Judge Dickerson of the Denver District Court had shown up for an honest return on taxpayers' dollars, and there was still no sign of the tall, tanned drink of water in that coffee-brown and pancaked Stetson, tobacco-tweed suit, and low-heeled cavalry boots they'd told the assassin about. So where in blue blazes could that big U.S. deputy marshal working out of the Denver Federal Building *be* as the summer sun rose ever higher in the thin dry air above the mile-high capital of Colorado and the tarred roofing-felt all around commenced to heat up considerably?

In point of fact, U.S. Deputy Marshal Custis Long was enjoying a late breakfast in bed with a piano teacher who liked to give French lessons over on Logan Street. Longarm, as he was better known to his pals as well as the rooftop assassin out to gun him at the moment, had *meant* to get to work on time that morning, but seeing that Miss Flora Lee had seemed so scared at the sight of his considerable naked height suddenly looming over her by the dawn's early light, he'd felt he owed such a gracious hostess a reassuring cuddle and more formal good-bye, which, in bed with the warm-natured Flora Lee, had naturally led to more time than you could shake a stick at slipping away. And so, seeing he was going to get hell when he got to the office in any case, where in the U.S. Constitution did it say you could fire a hand for eating breakfast in bed after you'd already fired him for showing up so late for work again?

Serving his tray of scrambled eggs and marmalade on buttered toast, with genuine Arbuckle Brand coffee black as sin and stronger than her willpower, the pleasantly plump piano teacher seemed suddenly somehow less modest, with her dark wavy hair unbound to her trim waist and that apron she'd slipped on to protect her bare hide from breakfast stove-splatters offering her perky nipples a sort of fence to peek over as it lay in interesting crumples in her otherwise bare lap. It sure beat all how gazing down on familiar scenery from a differant angle could inspire such renewed interest. But as he polished off the eggs and washed some toast down with her inspiring black coffee, Longarm regretfully declared, "That was swell. But if I don't make it to the office by ten, this time Marshal Vail has vowed to fire me, and the Federal Building's a good six- or eight-block run from here!"

As she set the tray aside and shucked her apron, she coyly suggested that he'd be running downhill most of the way, and seeing she'd taken the matter in hand as she forked a lush thigh across him, six or eight blocks didn't seem all that far as long as they made this the last time for certain.

And so, as the cathedral chimes atop Capitol Hill tolled ten A.M. to catch Longarm tearing across Broadway at the bottom of the rise, the assassin laying for him across

2

from the Federal Building gave up for the time being and rose to abandon such an unprofitable position for another they'd also mentioned.

So the assassin was moving down the stairwell of that transient rooming house across the way as Longarm legged it up the granite steps of the Federal Building, ducking inside just as the assassin was casually stepping outside to saunter innocently down the rooming house steps, and then west along the sandstone walk with a desperately casual glance at that list of Denver addresses supplied by a really desperate client.

Pausing outside the oaken door to get his breath under control with the help of a three-for-a-nickel cheroot, Longarm pasted an innocent smile across his weathered features and went on in as if he always reported for work after ten A.M.

It didn't seem to be working. Young Henry, the prissy squirt who played the typewriter and wrangled the filing cabinets out front, gave Longarm a "Now you're gonna get it!" look, but tried to sound sympathetic as he warned, "The boss has company in the back. From Washington. So move in slow and sensible."

Longarm nodded and replied, "*Muchas gracias, amigo mío*. What sort of a mood might good old Billy Vail be in this bright and sunny morn?"

Henry said, "Sore as hell. That bird from the main office got here hours ago, asking for you by name. You'd better get back there on the double, but like I said, behave yourself for a change!"

So Longarm ambled on toward the inner sanctum of their boss, Marshal Billy Vail, cocked his Stetson at a proper cavalry trim, and went in to take his medicine.

A portly middle-aged gent in a summer-weight seer-sucker suit sat in the only guest chair across a cluttered desk from the even older and chunkier Billy Vail. The banjo clock on one oak-paneled wall said it was going on five past ten. But old Billy just nodded his bullet head and declared, without taking the thick black stogie from between his teeth, "Here's our wandering boy now. I take it Dinty Flynn was no longer with us when you and the boys swept the stockyards like I told you this morning?"

"I ain't even certain he came back to Denver after busting out of Canyon City, Boss," Longarm replied truthfully, once one studied on it. He had no idea what Billy Vail was talking about.

His boss said, "We can let the Denver Police worry about *that* road agent. Old Dinty's never killed anybody yet. This here would be Field Supervisor Wortham from the Census Bureau, Custis. They asked for our help with a more dedicated night rider."

Supervisor Wortham rose to shake hands as he explained, "The Constitution of these United States calls for us to tally up the population every ten years, and it's tough enough when our riders are allowed to visit remote homesteads unmolested. We've been given to understand you've cracked more than one tough case out west in Utah Territory. You seem to have Mormons, Paiutes, and Shoshones scared of you."

Longarm could have told the older man you caught more flies with honey than with vinegar, and addressed Mormons as Saints and withheld comment on their peculiar notions about coffee, tea, and marriage. But with the clock on the wall pointing those accusing hands at him, he figured the less he said, the better.

So sure enough, Billy Vail calmly told Longarm, "Two census-takers have been drygulched so far, with this year's census barely under way out in the Great Basin now that the spring thaw's dried up. Needless to say, both of 'em were working for the U.S. government when they

4

were assassinated whilst on duty, making it federal, and it gets worse."

Wortham sat back down, leaving Longarm the only one there on his feet as Wortham told him, "We've asked for you, or some other federal man who knows the Mormon Delta better than most honest men, because we haven't been able to get a word out of those clannish cultists out yonder. To hear them tell, our two murdered census-takers, Corman and Lescot, barely talked to any member of the cult before they were first warned to turn around and go home, and then shot in two separate incidents on open range when they wouldn't!"

Longarm thoughtfully asked, "How do we know this, seeing nobody out yonder has come forward as a witness?"

Wortham nodded at Vail and observed, "You're right. He's good." Then he told Longarm, "Vince Corman wired a report on his own encounter with the assassin, or the assassin's messenger, at any rate. Corman was warned riding back to Ogden after a fruitless day in the saddle. He wired that few of the Mormon settlers he'd tried to tally up had been willing to answer his simple questions, and that then he'd been stopped on the road and warned in no uncertain terms that he'd live a lot longer if he just boarded the next eastbound over the South Pass and left God's Chosen People to dwell in peace along the banks of the Jordan."

Longarm murmured, "Well, they do call that freshwater creek running into the Great Salt Lake from the east the River Jordan. But most of 'em consider themselves the Latter-Day Saints and suspect the Indians of being long-lost Israelites. Did Vince Corman *describe* this bird who tried in vain to scare him off?"

Wortham nodded. But it was Billy Vail who said, "That might have been why a census-taker in his teens

5

wasn't scared off. He described a road agent all in black, holding a Harrington and Richardson .32, and seated sidesaddle."

Longarm smiled dubiously and quietly asked, "Did the rider she was out to terrify say whether she was *pretty* or not?"

Wortham said, "She was dressed in a sort of monk's habit, or maybe I should say a *nun's* habit, with her face covered by a pointed hood. But Colman wired that she sounded like a young woman of some refinement, in spite of her promise to kill him in cold blood the next time they met. Corman wired that in, allowed he was arming himself with a Remington Repeater, and that was the last we heard of him until a U.P. trackwalker who wasn't a Mormon because he was of the colored persuasion noticed a whole lot of carrion crows, and ambled on over through the sage to find what was left of poor Vince Corman. He'd been dead at least three days, according to the railroad police. Young Nick Lescot was found not long after, albeit he'd been dead longer, by some Western Union linemen an hour's ride out of Ogden the other way."

Vail opined, "It almost looks as if they wanted their bodies to be found. Be easy as pie to hide a body for keeps out amid all those arid sage and salt flats. But then they'd have to scare off all the outsiders who came searching for their missing pals."

Longarm asked, "What happened to their horses? If they arrived by rail, they'd have hired mounts at some livery in Ogden, right?"

Marshal Vail beamed at Wortham and boasted, "I told you he knew his onions. What'll you bet he opens with a bid on those Mormon ponies?"

The Washington-based Wortham didn't seem to be following their drift. Longarm resisted the impulse to ask

6

whether everyone back East had taken to those new-fangled bicycles, and simply explained, "When you hire a mount at any livery stable, they expect you to bring it back sooner or later."

Wortham brightened and said, "Oh, I see! When Corman and his fellow census-taker were blown out of their saddles, their livery mounts should have been reported missing, unless they were returned by somebody else or wandered home on their own."

Longarm nodded soberly and said, "I'll ask around as soon as I get out there. What makes us so certain the other census-taker, Nick Lescot, met up with that mysterious gal in black?"

Wortham replied easily, "They were both examined in Ogden by a deputy coroner of the Hebrew persuasion. As you no doubt know, the railroad town of Ogden is about the only settlement of any size in the Utah Territory that's not run lock, stock, and barrel by the Salt Lake Temple. So that's how we know both those lads were shot in the back by the same gun."

Longarm thoughtfully asked, "That bitty .32 whore pistol, on open range?"

Wortham sniffed and said, "Of course not. An Army-issue Springfield .45-70 with a killing range of close to a country mile."

Longarm whistled softly and decided, "High-power .45-70 would do a man dirty from distant cover. But the Army Springfield Conversions ain't the only rifles chambered for such rounds. So let's keep an open mind and simply say the lady never drygulched anybody with that whore pistol. It's too early to say whether she gunned a living soul or not. Like the old church song says, farther along, we'll know more about it."

\*　　\*　　\*

7

In the meantime, the rooftop assassin who'd given up on the Federal Building had dropped by Longarm's rooming house on the unfashionable side of Cherry Creek with a fake message from Billy Vail, asking when they might expect him back at the office.

Longarm's motherly and sincerely puzzled landlady allowed she'd be proud to give her occasional boarder the message when and if he ever showed up there again. But since Longarm had in fact been on a roll with that piano teacher, and earlier that vaudeville dancer who'd been mighy fond of Denver, his befuddled landlady allowed in all sincerity that he might be off on some field mission. They were wont to send him all over creation, she confided, accounting for his odd nickname, a play on his given name and the long arm of the law.

So the assassin from the Utah Territory legged it on over to the Union Station to discreetly question the head ticket agent, posing as a Pinkerton agent who had to contact the federal lawman in a hurry.

As luck would have it, since Longarm was still on his way home to pack before he tried to catch that after-supper combination to Ogden he'd caught before, nobody at the Union Station had seen hide or hair of him that morning. But since Longarm *had* run up to Leadville and back by rail less than a week earlier, one of the ticket agents, when pressed, recalled, "Hold on. I think I might have sold that tall dark drink of water a ticket . . . let's see . . . yesterday or the day before."

So the paid assassin went next to the nearby Western Union, to send a coded message warning that, as they'd feared, the Census Bureau had beaten them to the punch in Denver and that the one Gentile with a badge who'd made enough Mormon friends to matter had already left and could be most anywhere in the Utah Territory by this late date!

Then, not knowing about that passenger-freight combination leaving after dark, the assassin headed for cover at the Dexter Hotel, meaning to stay out of sight until it might be safe to board that Burlington Flier later in the day.

Knowing they'd expect it, whether it was a long shot or not, the assassin sent to head Longarm off resolved to get to the station a tad early that afternoon, in the unlikely event Longarm hadn't left Denver days earlier.

That was a shrewd enough guess about a federal employee who wasn't paid enough to pay for express tickets when he could bum free rides from the friendly conductor of a slower night train. So as his would-be assassin covered the Union Station in vain that afternoon, Longarm was in point of fact enjoying coffee and cake with a sweet young thing over on Lincoln Street. The baggage and Winchester '73 from his boardinghouse reposed in her kitchen as they enjoyed first the coffee and cake, and then each other, in her front parlor. Her name was Tilly, her hair was the color of fresh corn-silk, and he had to allow that whether she carried on as wild as Flora Lee or not, she carried on wild enough, and what the hell, he had a train to catch that evening.

# Chapter 2

Longarm had signed on with the Justice Department six or eight years earlier after discovering that a junior deputy made more on the job than a top cowhand. By the time President Rutherford B. Hayes got elected on a reform ticket and decreed prim-and-proper dress for a federal lawman to report for work in, Longarm had tallied up too much seniority to just quit and go back to punching cows in sensible work duds.

But as he boarded the caboose of that night combination bound for the Utah Territory with his battered McClellan saddle, Winchester '73, and other possibles, he felt sure neither President Hayes nor his fussy First Lady, Miss Lemonade Lucy, were watching owl-eyed in the gathering dusk. So he'd changed to a more practical field outfit of clean but faded blue denim jeans and jacket, with a hickory shirt and a loosely knotted kerchief, instead of that prissy shoestring necktie they required on the paved streets of Denver these days.

He had no way of knowing anyone was on the prod for a lawman of his size and build who was packing a cross-draw double-action Colt .44-40 under a frock coat of tobacco tweed. But whether they'd told him to work in secret or not, his own free choice of traveling wear allowed him to drop off with his baggage in the Ogden railyards with nobody he was interested in, or vice versa, any the wiser.

The railroads swapping freight and passengers amid the confusion of their consolidated yards ran what amounted to a company town as well. But if Ogden itself was run by outsiders, the officials of the surrounding county were members in good standing of the Church of Jesus Christ of Latter-Day Saints. Starting with the county sheriff.

Longarm didn't care. A spell back, traveling through as a bodyguard for Miss Sarah Bernhardt on orders from the State Department, Longarm had wrangled box seats for the show for the sheriff and his wives. So after introducing his two younger wives as his sisters-in-law, the older Utah lawman had allowed he owed such a neighborly Gentile a favor, should one ever be asked.

Mormons called most everyone who wasn't a Saint a Gentile. Some Jewish riders Longarm knew seemed to find that sort of confusing.

The slow but steady passenger-freight combination had taken all night and change to drop him and his baggage off in Ogden, but it was still early for courtesy calls. So Longarm toted his load to a clean but inexpensive hotel near the yards, and hired a room for himself and that heavily laden Army saddle. He draped it over the brass foot of the bed, locked up, and wedged a match stem under the bottom hinge, out in the empty hall, before he went downstairs to enjoy forbidden black coffee and stock up on plenty of smokes at the lobby newsstand, having learned the hard way how tough it could be to buy liquor, tobacco, or other stimulants anywhere else in the Mormon Delta.

That was what they called the more settled part of the Utah Territory. An awesome amount of the territory was still uncertainly mapped country—high verging on alpine, and low verging on arid desert beyond the call of duty.

The irrigated and more settled Morman Delta wasn't much like the famous Nile Delta, which was shaped like the Greek letter delta all the other deltas were named after. Few other deltas were shaped that way. The Mormon Delta wasn't just those big green patches where the Bear, the Jordan, and other mountain streams ran into the Great Salt Lake. The first settlers had started thereabouts, but working like beavers with a better grasp of the subject and plenty of mules to push their famous backward Mormon plows, they'd dammed, ditched, and graded way the hell south along the western slopes of the Continental Divide to form a wide green band of well-watered agriculture that only looked modest in proportion to one hell of an arid Great Basin, with fair-sized beef herds grazing the marginal range as far from water as most cows could manage back and forth. So those poor census-takers had been set almost hopeless chores even before that side-saddle assassin had called a sudden halt to their thankless efforts.

Longarm knew lots of folks from other lands, and folks just plain dumb about the U.S. Constitution, resented the whole notion of answering personal questions from total strangers who might be out to tax a poor but honest country boy who had enough damned troubles on his plate.

Since Longarm read a lot for a country boy from West-by-God-Virginia, he understood why the Founding Fathers had empowered federal riders to be so nosy. Every state rated two Senators no matter how many folks occupied it. But to balance that, the House of Representatives was made up of members speaking for

12

Congressional districts of about the same population and, to manage that, the gents setting up each new congress had to know about how many folks there might be in each and every district.

There was just no way to slice the pie fairly unless they took a pesky census every ten years, like Washington, Jefferson, and others had thought they should.

As he put a socially unacceptable cheroot aside and stepped outside, Longarm had a tougher time with the motives of that mystery gal with the .32 whore pistol, backed by a .45-70. The late Vince Corman had described her voice and accent as educated. So there went the notion of stubborn trash whites who didn't want to discuss living in sin with their sisters. Ignorant country folk, however ornery, hardly ever hired smooth-talking mysterious strangers to do their fighting for them. Trash whites and cranky hermits *wanted* everybody to know about it on those rare occasions when they actually won a fight. So anybody smooth enough to hire some educated woman, however sinister, to first warn off and later back up her threats with murder in cold blood, had to have some sensible *motive*, and that was where Longarm kept getting bogged down.

There were crazy-mean killers everywhere. But the powerful Mormon elders running everything these days had been busting a gut trying to patch things up with Washington in order to become a state. A state's got to govern itself more than a territory with a federally appointed governor. So when you pictured all those saints in the most selfish possible light they'd have to see, if they had a lick of sense, how shooting federal census-takers would be as smart as shooting their fool selves in their feet.

He ran the notion of statehood backward to see if that might take him somewhere as he strode on toward Ogden's smaller version of the Denver Federal Building. He'd never enjoyed cleaning out the chicken coops back home in West-by-God-Virginia either. But when they set you a chickenshit chore, it was best to just go ahead and get it over with.

So he went on up to the office of Billy Vail's opposite number with the Ogden District Court, and entered to confront the opposite number of prissy Henry, a not-much-older and sort of piggy squirt wearing sleeve garters and a green eyeshade as he stared morosely up from behind his own typewriting machine.

When Longarm introduced himself, the piggy priss looked shocked and asked, "Are you accustomed to reporting for duty in Denver dressed like some sort of border ruffian, Deputy Long?"

To which Longarm could only reply, "I ain't allowed to. I ain't reporting for duty anywhere at the moment. On orders from the boss I *work* for, I've come to pay a courtesy call on this here federal outfit. But if you don't feel I'm pretty enough, I'll just go on about my field mission and you can go to hell."

The clerk typist hastily suggested it might be best if he were to announce a lawman from another jurisdiction to his *own* boss. So Longarm told him to snap to it, and sure enough, the piggy priss came back with an invitation to yet another inner sanctum.

Neither that piggy priss nor the Marshal Dixler running this office now had been here the last time Longarm had passed through. But the wiry, gray Dixler said to call him Abe, and broke out some two-bit cigars as he offered his visitor a seat and resumed his own at a desk that seemed a litter-mate of old Billy Vail's, complete with the clutter of onionskins and yellow Western Union messages scattered across it.

Longarm lit the not-bad smoke to give himself time to

choose his words before he declared, "I hope it's understood that neither my boss, Marshal Vail, nor anyone else
from the Denver office had any say in my being assigned
to the case of those two census riders, sir."

Marshal Dixler replied, "I told you to call me Abe. It's
no skin off my ass if you Denver riders get to chase your
tails around in circles over this way. I can tell you why
the Census Bureau dealt you in and us out. I *signed* the
night letter informing Washington we hadn't been able
to cut any trail or get one Mormon witness to offer us
an educated guess when we canvased a day's ride north
and south."

Longarm blew a thoughtful smoke ring and suggested,
"To call somebody a witness, you have to assume they
saw something. I have often found that folks who haven't
seen anything seem reluctant to tell me they saw something. But whilst you and your own hands were canvasing, did anybody think to ask about the livery mounts
those two dead boys should have been riding when they
were drygulched?"

The older lawman looked disgusted and suggested,
"They might have been taking that census on roller
skates, but I'll allow ponies seem more sensible, if you'll
allow me to inform you that not one of the eight livery
stables in town or the Army remount section out to Fort
Douglas would own up to one missing mount. Somebody
has to be lying, of course. I can't see the War Department
or the five Gentile livery outfits in this railroad town covering up for Mormon killers. But I don't have a thing
pointing to any one of the three Mormon livery men."

He snorted smoke out both nostrils like a fighting bull
before he added, "I swear, those religious fanatics have
been bred to lie even when the truth is in their favor!
When you ask them why on earth any honest man would
want to prevent a simple head count of the local popu-

lation, they give you this dreamy smile and stare through you, as if they know something you don't know and they ain't about to tell you!"

Longarm suggested, "I've been thinking about those census forms. There's more to them than a simple head count. Over the years a whole lot of other federal agencies have added questions of their own to what started out less complicated. Interior wants the Census Bureau to fill them in some on land management. The War Department likes to hear local opinions on Mister Lo, the Poor Indian, and so on, to the point where some might feel pressed. I mean, where do you draw the line bewixt asking how many water pumps or how many whiskey stills you might have on your quarter section?"

Marshal Dixler snorted, "Mormons don't have whiskey stills on their claims."

Longarm nodded soberly and pointed out, "Few if any hold claims under the federal Homestead Act of '62. I mean to ask just how they portioned out the land amongst the congregation when they first came over the South Pass back when all this land belonged to Mexico. As for few if any distilling moonshine, that ain't the only sort of family business some old-time Mormons might not care to discuss with any outsiders."

Dixler nodded knowingly and said, "You're talking about polygamy. We've been assured the Salt Lake Temple frowns on the practice these days. That's not saying any Mormon lawman is about to arrest a soul for practicing it. But wouldn't it make more sense to just fib about that to a census-taker? Neither Corman nor Lescot were armed with search warrants or backed by an armed escort. Killing a visitor is sure to attract more attention than just describing all the women on a spread as a sewing bee and sending the snoop on his way, right?"

Longarm nodded, saying, "That's the way I see it. So

16

the person or persons who blocked this summer's census, for the moment, must have been afraid those fairly green young riders were about to stumble onto something more noticeable than an extra wife or two."

When Abe Dixler asked what that might have been, Longarm was forced to admit, "I sure wish you hadn't asked that. I just don't know. But I mean to ask that mystery woman in black as soon as I meet up with her."

Abe Dixler cocked a bushy gray brow and observed, "I see you've been reading those whoppers about your tracking skills in that fool *Denver Post*. How do you propose to catch up with her at this late date, seeing she got away clean with all the time in the world to change out of that spooky costume, and the only man on our side who might recognize her voice is on his way back East in a lead-lined box?"

Longarm said, "It might not be bad as all that. I have one more call to make on a friendly Mormon lawman before I stick my neck out. He might know something I can use for bait instead."

The older federal lawman demanded, "What are you talking about? What sort of bait might draw that murderous sidesaddle assassin out of hiding, now that she's given us all the slip and has to know we're looking for her serious?"

Longarm replied simply, "Me. Unless I can come up with something better, soon enough to matter. If I can't find her, I'll have to let her come looking for me, and once she does . . ."

"That's why she *won't*," the older local lawman declared, adding, "Whoever she may be, she must have read those stories about you in the *Denver Post* too. Would either a gal riding sidesaddle with a whore pistol or the backshooter with a .45-70 she might be working with want to go up against a gunfighter with your rep on open range?"

Longarm decided. "They might try to ambush me somewhere safer. But they're going to have to try, unless they admit they murdered those two census-takers in vain."

Dixler shook his head wearily and demanded, "Get to the fool point! Anyone can see they assassinated those two kids to prevent them from taking a census along the Mormon Delta. But where does it say that they have to assassinate any lawman investigating their assassination?"

Longarm explained, "I asked Field Supervisor Wortham to issue me my own census forms. I have 'em in a saddlebag at my hotel. I ain't fixing to waste time hunting for their killer or killers. I aim to carry on on their place and finish their census for them."

Dixler whistled thoughtfully and said, "I follow your drift. If you can't find the bitch-wolf's den you can set a trap for her with your own back as the bait! She'll have to come after you or let you finish the job of those two kids she stopped! But we know she stopped Vince Corman whilst he was on the prod for someone to try. So what if she stops you, as well?"

To which Longarm could only reply, "Then I'll never speak to you again and it won't be my problem. So what the hell."

# Chapter 3

"She's sure to kill you!" the Mormon sheriff flatly decreed when Longarm met with him half an hour later. They were seated on a park bench in Courthouse Square for privacy. The sheriff hadn't been too clear as to whether the Saints in his office had to be kept in the dark about their conversation or their friendship. Marshal Dixler's remark about distant looks and knowing smiles had been on the money.

Dying for a smoke but minding his manners in public, Longarm could only reply, "She might not be working alone. Vince Corman had wired in about her threats and must have been on the prod for her. So what if another rider entirely rode within rifle range on a wide-open sage flat? Or what if she popped out of nowhere to distract him whilst a sidekick with that .45-70 drew a bead on his distracted back?"

The sheriff said, "What if there are fairies in the bottom of the garden? What name are you going to use as you try for them pretending to be another census-taker?"

Longarm replied, "My own. I asked Supervisor Wortham about that back in Denver. Census data gathered under false pretenses would be worthless. Any U.S. citizen who wants the job can ask the questions, but he or she has to sign his or her true name to the report."

The sheriff demurred, "But won't your whole point in covering the same ground as Corman and Lescot be aimed at catching their killer or killers? Evidence gathered by a lawman working incognito can be and is often presented in court, right?"

Longarm nodded, but said, "Still makes more sense to finish the census chores on the up and up. Uncle Sam will be able to use any data I collect whether I catch anybody or *they* nail *me,* and that Scotch poet who warned about the tangled webs we weave whilst trying to bullshit everybody had a point. I ain't exactly unknown out here in the Great Basin, and the killer or killers have to be expecting somebody like me to come sniffing for their sign. So it makes for less needless bullshit if I just admit what I'm doing to anybody that asks."

"You're going to get killed," the sheriff repeated. Then he sighed and declared, "The gals really enjoyed that show, and they're still bragging about you introducing them to the Divine Sarah after it was over. So you might as well know. We're pretty sure it was one killer, that sidesaddled woman in black, working alone. We're still working on how she came to have the Indian sign on the congregations north and south of the east-west rails. Before you ask, the Salt Lake Temple hasn't authorized any Danite activity since the Apostle Brigham died back in '77."

He glared at a pigeon on the walk and muttered, "Most of that stuff about Destroying Angels was made up by Gentile reporters anyhow!"

Longarm was too polite to bring up the leftover Danites he'd had his own troubles with in more recent times.

He knew the leaders of the Main Temple had never had complete control over neighborhood fanatics or bullies in some far corners of what they would have described as the State of Deseret if Washington hadn't decided on Utah Territory. He just asked, "What makes you say she has the Indian sign on anyone out yonder?"

The sheriff sighed and said, "Not anyone. *Everyone.* I'm an elder of my own temple, and all of my deputies are Saints. So it wasn't as if we were Gentile reporters, out to write another exposition about fair white maidens being held as love-slaves by Mormon sex maniacs. I mean, they're *allowed* to talk to *us!*"

Longarm said he followed the older lawman's drift, and he did. He knew how Brigham Young himself had been taken in by that English travel writer Richard Burton, who'd said he wanted to publish a true account of the new religious settlement near the Great Salt Lake and then, after being dined if not wined by his Mormon hosts, had gone home to write his sensational *City of the Saints*, with a heap of snide tongue-in-cheek observations about what had likely been a sort of tedious stay among hardworking carpenters and ditch-diggers who sang a lot. Other Saints had told Longarm they'd been advised, not commanded, to keep outsiders at a polite distance and neither lie nor volunteer anything that could be distorted into another sensational book about them.

When the sheriff just kept muttering under his breath, Longarm said, "What do you reckon they've been holding out on you, pard?"

The sheriff sighed and said, "If I knew, it wouldn't be a secret. When you ask, they naturally say they've nothing to hide. But take such simple matters as last visits and livery horses. I mean, since Corman was canvasing north of here whilst Lescot was visiting the spreads to the south, you'd think it would be easy enough to find

21

out who they'd pestered last with those census forms, right?"

Longarm nodded and pointed out, "None of the census figures they'd taken up to their deaths were found near their bodies. They might have been in their saddlebags."

The sheriff said, "I was getting to that. Where might those saddlebags, saddles, and two whole ponies be? Stealing stock is considered almost as bad as drygulching outsiders in these parts. Neither of those outsiders rode over the South Pass on their own ponies. So they must have hired or borrowed not one but two."

Longarm quietly observed, "Marshal Dixler mentioned drawing a blank at all the local liveries as well as Fort Douglas. When you shoot a man off a pony, one of two things has to happen. Somebody grabs the reins to lead the pony most anywhere, or the riderless pony heads home to its manger as soon as it feels hungry and thirsty enough. Hasn't anybody been able to describe what sort of riding stock those young census-takers might have been riding?"

The sheriff said, "If they had, we might have tracked one or more back to its owner by now. The Saints who might or might not have had a few words or even *seen* Corman or Lescot can't be certain."

Longarm objected, "Corman had been running his census north of town for days before he wired about that spooky lady telling him to stop."

The sheriff replied, "I just said that. They're scared skinny or they've something bigger than a double murder to hide out yonder! Since I can't think of anything Saints in good standing with their church might be up to, that mystery woman in black must have some stronger hold over them."

Longarm hesitated, chose his words carefully, and quietly suggested, "There was this out-of-the-way congregation, over to the far side of your Great Salt Desert near the Nevada line. I was later assured your Salt Lake Temple hadn't even known it was there. So there was this bearded wonder lording it over his armed and dangerous followers with new revelations direct from the Angel Moroni, and I don't mind telling you they had me worried for a spell."

The sheriff quietly replied, "I heard about you escaping to the outside world across the salt flats. That was out yonder. We're here on the Delta within earshot of the transcontinental railroad engines. I'm an elder of our church, for Pete's sake. Don't you reckon I'd have heard if some false apostle had come forth with any teachings contrary to the Book of Mormon?"

"You say you're still working on the color of those horses the two murdered census-takers were riding?" Longarm asked dryly.

The sheriff protested, "That's not what I meant. I said, and I still say, somebody has those settlers too scared to talk to elders of their own church!"

Then he added, "I do know one thing. She rides alone. From somewhere closer to town. Can't get a thing about her out of any members of the church. But some colored kids from that railroad shantytown north of the consolidated yards told one of my deputies about what they took for a Klan rider, seated sidesaddle on a big black horse, tearing past in the gloaming light after supper time, when all good children shouldn't have been messing about along the U.P. drainage ditches. The crawdad-hunting colored kids said they'd spotted her riding alone in that spooky hooded outfit."

Longarm smiled thinly and said, "Now we're getting somewhere. Did those kids say whether she'd spotted *them* in the tricky light of the gloaming?"

The sheriff said, "They told my rider they'd ducked

down in the cattails along the ditch. Would she have ridden past there more than once if she'd thought she'd been spotted?"

Longarm shook his head and decided, "I'd best have a word with those kids before I pester any secretive Saints. Try her night riding this way. Ogden is a fair-sized town with a mixed population of your kind, my kind, and all sorts of oddities who seldom spit and wittle on the same steps. A woman of any breed or description could find it easy enough to keep to herself with any number of horses. Riding a black one through town in that black-robed outfit might attract some attention. But what if she just stepped out her back door after supper time for a ride in the cool of the evening while dressed more normal? What if she rode out of sight wearing, say, polka dots and a perky hat, to slip that black outfit on over her more innocent duds as she crossed the railroad yards in the gathering dusk?"

The sheriff said, "That would account for those colored kids spotting her coming their way at a gallop, all dressed up with something more spooky in mind. I wish I could get somebody to tell us where she rode after leaping that ditch on her handsome horse!"

Longarm said, "Horseflesh may be her undoing. I'll check with those more willing young witnesses, but unless they change their story, we're looking for a big black field hunter, along with those mystery mounts Corman and Lescot must have been riding."

The sheriff asked how Longarm made the one those kids had spotted a hunter, seeing it had been described as close to a thoroughbred.

Longarm said, "No thoroughbred would have jumped a ditch as wide as the U.P. work gangs dig. The English hunting breeds are related to their regular racehorses and nigh as fast, but more lightly built and bred to take foolish chances over blind jumps. Our mystery woman knows what she's doing aboard such a mount in well-watered country. An Indian pony might have the edge on such fancy stock in rougher and drier country, but here in your flat and irrigated Delta there ain't no way to overtake that big field hunter with any brute less than another field hunter! It's the ditches you get to jump that she has in mind. Poor young Corman got that part wrong. She wasn't laying for him along the post road the way he wired. She moves cross country, going *over* ditches and fences cutting across her path, well off the regular roads."

He rose to his feet, smiling down at the older lawman as he added, "So you see, it's sort of like peeling onionskins away, one at a time. My boss, Marshal Vail, calls it the process of eliminating. I ain't left town yet and I've a better picture of our sidesaddle assassin and the way she's been getting about in that spooky outfit."

His sudden movement to his feet had been unexpected by the rooftop sniper across Courthouse Square. So the .45-70 slug meant for Longarm's heart plowed into the backrest of their bench to shower the sheriff with green-painted slivers as Longarm, spotting the powder smoke against the roof edge, crabbed to one side as a second round buzzed like an angry hornet through the space he'd been standing in.

Then Longarm pegged a round of .44-40 from his six-gun through the smoke peeking over the roof edge at them as he hissed at the older lawman, "Cover me! I have her position!"

Then he was running across the square, with pigeons, kids, and nursemaids scattering out of his path as he zig-zagged some with his smoking gun in hand.

The rifle shots had come from the flat roof of an office building. That saved having to mess with introductions, and doubtless acounted for the other shootist's choice of positions.

So Longarm tore four stories up the winding stairwell unopposed, to kick open the door at the top, pop out fast to crab to one side, and feel his rectum pucker as he found himself too close to the edge for comfort.

It was obvious the rifle shooter had been prone atop the tar paper without even a low parapet between his or her position and a long way down. That explained why Longarm's answering pistol fire had inspired second thoughts. The two spent cartridges near the edge of the roof read a hasty retreat as well. But just in case, Longarm moved around to the far side of the stairwell shed and under the water tank to make sure he had the whole rooftop to himself now.

The Mormon sheriff, who'd lived through his own share of gunplay in his time, was smart enough to call out before he opened the sheet-metal door to join the younger lawman with his own Navy Colt Conversion in hand.

Longarm dryly remarked, "Long gone. I zigged all them zags for nothing. He, she, or it was ducking down the stairs as I was running across the plaza. I hate it when they do that."

The Mormon sheriff said, "Nobody downstairs saw anything. I asked on the way up. Everyone's out in the halls now. They were all at their desks when the shooting started, or so they say."

Longarm bent to pick up and pocket the spent brass as he replied, "We were talking about whether I ought to conduct that census under an assumed name?"

The local lawman sighed and said, "She doesn't want you to have a better picture of her. She knows that you're here. She knows you're looking for her. She just proved she knows what you look like, and you wouldn't know her on sight if you woke up in bed with her!"

Longarm smiled crookedly and replied, "I doubt my boss would want me to wake up in bed with her. But don't his process of eliminating beat all?"

When the older lawman seemed sincerely puzzled, Longarm explained, "Look what she's given away just now. She's just told us she knows they've sent me after her. So she must know Vince Corman wired that description of her. She has to know that the Census Bureau asked for me by name, or she'd have had no call to assassinate me just now. Like I said, process of eliminating!"

The Mormon sheriff grimaced and pointed out, "You're the one who figures to be eliminated, at the rate you're going! Sure, she failed this time. But she got away clean, and we still have no idea who she might be or what she might look like! What if she tries again?"

Longarm shrugged and said, "I purely hope she does. I figure that would be a swell way to catch her!"

# Chapter 4

The livery stable closest to the railroad depot was one of those run by Mormons. Longarm toted his McClellan, laden with saddlebags and saddled-booted Winchester, in to their rental office and told them their Mormon sheriff had recommended them. The old Saint in bib overalls seemed quietly pleased, and allowed they could fix him up with a swell mount for two bits a day plus a ten-dollar deposit.

As he followed the older man around to the corral with his saddle, Longarm casually mentioned those other federal riders, Corman and Lescot. If the old Saint knew anything, he wasn't saying. He didn't sound interested as he allowed that both federal and county lawmen had already questioned him about those Gentile boys. It was easy to lose track of strange faces, but he wasn't missing any riding stock. So it made no sense for Longarm to ask him what sort of stock the dead census-takers might have ridden out of town aboard.

Longarm chose a jug-headed paint that would be easy to describe, and once they'd saddled it and settled up, forked a long leg across the sort of low-slung pony to do

28

some riding as a distant church bell chimed eleven A.M. So he made it out to nearby Camp Ogden well before mess call, and reined in out front of the provost marshal's office.

Camp Ogden was an outpost of the bigger Fort Douglas to the south, and served as both a remount station and a military police post with an eye on transcontinental military traffic. There were no walls, but a heap of corral poles, with the provost marshal's office in front of the prison stockade about as impressive a building as they had.

He found the field-grade officer he'd come to see just fixing to leave for the officers' mess. Lieutenant Colonel Walthers didn't look at all happy to see Longarm. The last time they'd tangled, Longarm had knocked him on his ass.

"You've some nerve coming here where I'm in command!" snapped the tall and well-built, but somehow sissy-looking, short colonel. Longarm was sure the feelings of distaste were mutual. So as they stood there bristled up like angry dogs to the confusion of the desk sergeant, Longarm said, "Before you cloud up and rain all over me, I'm here to offer some tit for tat, Colonel. I neither know nor care why they transferred you out this way since our last waltz on the far side of South Pass. But I'm here on the case of those two assassinated census-takers you surely must have heard about."

Walthers stiffly replied, "One of your fellow deputy marshals was out here asking about horses. He suggested that since those census-takers were on federal business, we might have supplied them with some federal riding stock. We, I mean our remount officer, Major Haskell, assured him no military riding stock could be involved in the case. And now, if you'd be good enough to get the fuck out of my way, I'll be on my way to the officers' mess. I'd invite you to join me, but they don't serve saddle tramps at a table reserved for officers and gentlemen!"

Longarm replied, "That's all right. I never eat saddle tramps, and you really are the asshole of creation, Colonel! Hasn't it sunk in yet how much better you'd have come out on paper had you gone along with me instead of bucking me the times we've tangled over disputed jurisdiction?"

Interested in spite of himself, the imperious officer demanded, "What disputed jurisdiction did you have in mind this time? From the way it seems to me, the murder of two civilian federal employees by a person or person unknown, on or about a county road, would hardly be a military police matter!"

Longarm said, "Post road, federal, north and south of the tracks, and like you just said, federal employees. But I ain't asking you or any other soldier blue to help me bring their killer or killers to justice. I'm only asking for a little help in catching up with at least one rider mounted on a black brute I suspect of being a field hunter. There ain't no way I'll ever give such a mount and rider a run for the money aboard any scrub pony or even your average cavalry mount. I need something better. In return I'll be proud to write you up for assisting in the arrest and you'll never have to do toad squat."

Aware of his desk sergeant's interest, Colonel Walthers murmured, "Let's continue this interesting discussion outside. You can tell me what you have in mind on my way to the officers' mess."

But they never got there that day. By the time they were halfway across the parade ground, Longarm had filled in the snooty but not too slow self-seeker on just what he needed and what the advantages to all concerned might be. So Walthers said, "We're going to have to clear it with a junior officer, and *he's* going to want you to write him up for an assist as well. But I'm sure we have just the mount you need."

They did. The high-stepping slate-gray gelding they danced out of a stall for Longarm's inspection stood sixteen hands at the withers and answered to the name of Skylark. Officers got to buy their own arms, uniforms, and personal mounts. So Skylark, a field hunter who'd chased foxes in the Virginia Tidewater Country to hear tell, was the property of that Captain Spooner they'd sent for. When he wasn't hunting foxes, Captain Spooner worked for the post engineers.

It might have been rude to look a *gift* horse in the mouth, but as long as he'd offered tit for tat, Longarm felt he had a right to take a peek at Skylark's teeth.

They weren't too discouraging. They told him the big hunter was going on eight. The discolored slit you called Galvayne's groove, after the vet who'd first studied it seriously, was just peeking out of Skylark's gums to hint he was closer to ten. But his incisors still read more middle-aged than ancient, so farther long, as the song said, they'd know more about that.

First he had to get permission from the big hunter's rightful owner, and to Longarm's relief, the junior officer, once he showed up, proved a lot easier to get along with than old Colonel Walthers. Almost everybody in the U.S. Army was.

So they all shook on it, and Longarm asked if he could board his livery paint with them until he and Skylark came back.

When the sensible post engineer asked if it wouldn't save Longarm money to return the livery mount right off, Longarm explained he'd chosen to ride out of town on a distinctive scrub pony, and wanted it to stay that way for now.

Walthers was experienced enough to ask how Longarm knew the other side was watching for him around town.

Longarm said, "Somebody must have been. I never announced it in the morning papers that I'd be sitting in the open with the sheriff. But he, she, or it still managed to draw a bead on me with a .45-70, and by the way, does anybody make a newer rifle than your old Springfield Conversion for that Army round?"

It was the military police officer, to give the devil his due, who volunteered, "Winchester makes a show-off special chambered for five extra grains of powder. Bullard makes a repeater chambered for cheap and available Army rounds. Remington's new Keene Magazine rifle comes in any caliber you'd care to order, and as I said, the surplus Army .45-70 comes cheap as well as powerful."

So Longarm allowed he'd keep an eye peeled for most any brand of rifle aimed his way, and swapped his saddle to Skylark's higher back to see how the old field hunter felt about some rough riding.

Figuring he had the whole afternoon to work with, Longarm rode east toward the Wasatch Mountains, before he reined south to circle wide as far as the bare flats between the railroad center and the Great Salt Lake. Aside from scattered clumps of salt weed, the soil was sun-crazed and dusty where it rose well above the water table, or briny and slimy where it didn't. There were no trails across the treacherous footing because nobody rode that close to the shifty lake shores without good reason, and when one had a good reason, the flats were diced all to hell by drainage canals. Everything around the Ogden railroad yards spread across a flat lowland that called for lots of drainage.

So after Longarm had ridden Skylark across enough solid and soupy footing to trust him better, he heeled the big hunter into a gallop toward a brine-filled ditch about a yard below grade and a fathom wide.

Skylard sailed across it to land running without breaking stride, and seemed to be laughing back as Longarm heeled him on faster at a dead run, yelling, *"Bueno,* let's see what you can *do,* old hoss! If this was a steeplechase course and we were in the lead, would you let anybody catch up with us?"

It appeared Skylark wouldn't have, unless something faster than hell was on their heels. They were moving so fast across the flats that Longarm almost missed the next ditch ahead before Skylark was suddenly leaping it, nearly leaving his rider way in the middle of the air. But Longarm was a good rider aboard a good horse. So they got along fine and had a lot of fun before Longarm reined in to pat the warmed-up gelding's neck and declare, "We'd best save some for later, old hoss. We've worked north of the rooftops of Ogden, and I aim to lay for that sidesaddle assassin on that other hunter near the stretch those colored kids spotted her at twilight, see?"

Skylark didn't argue. They crossed a spur track west of the main yards, and worked their way east along it toward that shantytown he'd not only been told about, but knew from an earlier visit.

The transcontinental rails had been laid from the west by Chineese, and from the east by Irish, to meet in the Utah Territory over to the northwest at Promontory Point. But now that the rails had been laid, the tracks were mostly *walked* by colored work crews, and the Pullman porters were colored as well, calling for colored quarters all along the transcontinental lines, whether such folks were welcome or not.

The Book of Mormon allowed that the American Indians were members of the Lost Tribes of Israel, as long as they behaved themselves, but didn't say much, good or bad, about colored folks. So the discreetly located shantytown of colored railroad help wasn't there when you looked at the official surveys of the county. But as he rode Skylark in that afternoon, he couldn't help noticing that the informal sprawl of cinder-paved lanes had grown some since his last visit, or that more than one former shack had been spruced up with store-bought siding or a new roof of elephant iron.

There was no discreet way for a strange white man to pound on doors across a colored settlement. But if he remembered right, there was a small shack dispensing candy, liquor, tobacco, stove oil, and with any luck, gossip.

So he found his way there, dismounted as a quartet of small kids stared thunderstruck, and bet the biggest one a nickel he couldn't keep other kids from pestering his horse while he had a word inside.

Once he'd lost that bet, he tethered Skylark out front, took his Winchester '73 with him lest it prove too tempting, and strode on in to find the place empty save for a gal behind the counter in the gloom.

To his mild surprise, once he moved closer, she looked more like a full-blood Indian than a colored lady. Likely Paiute, judging from her short stature and pleasant moon face.

He told her who he was and explained he wanted a word with those kids who'd said they'd seen that woman in black riding hell for leather in the gloaming over to the east.

The Indian gal said, "I've been waiting a long time for you to get here. A county deputy was here earlier. He said the sheriff has been looking all over for you, and that we should tell you if you came by to ask about the Willard brothers. I can send for them if you like. But the

34

sheriff said it was important. I think I would go back to town right now if I were you!"

Longarm swore under his breath and declared, "I'd think so too if only I hadn't gone to a whole lot of trouble with that big field hunter out front. I didn't want anybody in town to know I was riding it. I still don't want anybody to know. But I reckon I could leg it back across the railroad yards if you'd be willing to hide Skylark for me out this way."

She smiled and replied, "I can do better than that. What if I tied your bigger mount out back and let you ride one of *our* ponies in to see what the sheriff wants?"

Longarm nodded eagerly, asked if she might by any chance have a paint to hire out to him, and when she allowed she did, asked how much he'd owe her for the favor.

The moonfaced gal looked hurt and murmured, "A favor is not a favor if you pay for it. You don't remember me, do you?"

To which Longarm was forced to honestly reply, "I'm sure I ought to, ma'am. But to tell the pure truth—"

"*You* all look alike to *us*," she cut in with a weary smile. "I wasn't wearing any clothes, but there were other girls with bigger tits all around that day you saved us all, up along the river you call the Bear."

When Longarm didn't answer, she declared, "It was the summer Buffalo Horn went crazy and led the Bannock out against your kind. You were scouting ahead for the blue sleeves when some of them came upon us with red thoughts and drawn sabers. I think they would have killed us, all of us, if you had not ridden between us waving your hat to shout that we were not Bannock. When a three-striped chief laughed and said any dead Indian was a good Indian, you said you were going to make a good Bohunk out of him. What is a Bohunk?"

Longarm laughed as that tense discussion in a Paiute camp on the banks of the Bear came back to him. He said, "Sergeant Novak was a second-generation Hunky from Bohemia, over to the Austro-Hungarian Empire. He went under fighting Ute along the White River not long after our discussion about you Paiute folk. You're commencing to look more familiar now that I picture you stark naked, no offense."

She smiled and said, "None taken. As you see, I have chosen to live less hand-to-mouth. Sometimes I miss our old free ways, but I never miss the hunger, or the cold, or getting shot at by both red and white . . . Bohunks for no reason. But come, I will show you around to the back so you can ride into town and find out what the sheriff wants. When you come back, we can talk about other favors I might do for a man I owe so much."

As he followed her out and around the shack, gathering Skylark along the way, Longarm felt obliged to mutter, "Aw, mush. It wasn't all that much. I doubt old Hunky Novak really meant to kill anybody."

To which she replied in an adoring tone, "Since he's dead, we'll never know. But I know he *didn't,* and I can still see how tall in the saddle and handsome you looked to me when you stood up for us for those frightening minutes that seemed to last forever!"

# Chapter 5

By the time they had Skylark hiding out in the small corral between the shack and her sleeping shanty, they'd established that she answered to the name of Hazel Mullroony and that her dad had been a mule skinner of the Hibernian persuasion for Overland. Her Paiute mom had been living white when Hazel had been born twenty-odd summers back. But when the late Dennis Mullroony had been taken by cholera, when Hazel had been eight or nine, her mom had taken her back to the free but far from easy life of her own digger band. So that accounted for Hazel's good English, her flexible approach to life, and that little lilt of Irish mischief in her Indian eyes.

As he singled out and saddled a runty paint cayuse from among her remuda of four, she explained how she'd come by them and this layout in a colored shantytown. Finding it tough to get any decent job in the white neighborhoods of Ogden, she'd gone to work for little more than room and board for the elderly colored widow who'd been left the place by her man, a railroad porter who'd saved up his tips. The elderly childless widow had taken a shine to her hardworking Indian helper, and left all she had to Hazel on her deathbed. The only fly in the ointment, according to Hazel, was feeling sort of awkward amid her colored customers and neighbors. Most seemed to accept her as simply peculiar. Others seemed to resent her as both a shopkeeper they had to ask for credit on occasion and, of course, an infernal *Indian*. White railroad workers weren't the only ones who'd ever been arrowed and scalped along the U.P. line.

Longarm said that they'd talk some more later, and asked if she could line up those three Willard brothers for him while he found out what the sheriff wanted. He explained, "I don't know how long I'll be in town. I want those boys to show me where they say they spotted that mystery woman I'm after. I might be able to head her off in the gloaming if she follows the same path across the yards at sundown."

Then he mounted up and rode the stubby paint across those very yards, noting how, by cutting back and forth around parked freight cars, a body entering the yards in one riding outfit might come out the far side robed in black.

He rode Hazel's paint to his hotel, and left it in their stable out back and across the alley. He asked at the desk if there were any wires or messages for him. The clerk handed him a note from the sheriff, adding that the deputy who'd left it had said it was urgent. Longarm read it as he went upstairs, saw by the match stem wedged in that bottom hinge that nobody had been messing with his hired room, and just took a piss down the hall before he headed on over to the sheriff's office.

This time they held their sit-down in a back room where nobody could peg shots at them from any distance. The sheriff told him a witness had come forward.

Reaching absently for a smoke, then remembering his

manners and the present company, Longarm buttoned his shirt flap instead as he asked whether the witness had volunteered information on Corman or Lescot.

The sheriff said, "Neither. He met up with that masked woman on the big black horse. She pointed her whore pistol at him and scared him out of a year's growth."

Longarm asked him to go on. So the sheriff explained, "Old Klaus Pommer is a Gentile, living here in town, but peddling tools and hardware from the East a day's haul north and south to Delta beef and produce growers. So it makes no sense to me neither, but Klaus Pommer swears that same sidesaddle assassin warned him at gunpoint he had till the end of the week to settle his affairs in the Utah Territory and vacate the premises forever, unless he meant to occupy a grave out our way until Judgment Day."

Longarm asked, "When does this Dutch peddler say that all this happened?"

The sheriff said, "This morning, around eight or nine, on the north post road where Corman was murdered. Pommer says he'd just driven his wagon out of sight from town when that spooky rider came up behind him out of nowhere, swung around to throw down on him, and delivered her short scary message in a high-toned ladylike way. How do you like that so far?"

Longarm frowned thoughtfully and declared, "I had things pictured different, but try her this way. Say the woman in black rode out of town at dusk, did some night riding nobody's told us about yet, and holed up out on the range with confederates, settlers she has the Indian sign on, or just under the stars on a dry summer night. Say that she knew that Dutch peddler's habits, laid for him to deliver her message, and then slipped into town just in time to peg those shots at us before noon."

The sheriff objected, "In broad daylight, dressed like

a spook on a big black horse, and nobody noticed?"

Longarm suggested, "If she spooked Pommer out of sight from anybody else, she could have easily slipped into something more innocent-looking and walked her mount in, pretending to be a town gal who'd been out for a morning canter or a farmer gal coming in to do some shopping."

The sheriff said he'd have his deputies canvas the shopkeepers and such over yonder if Longarm would be kind enough to suggest where yonder might be.

Longarm grimaced and said, "That's what I just said. She could have ridden in from any direction. I just proved, aboard another hunter, how a mount willing to do some jumping can carry you fast and far around this railroad center. Should one of your hands ask, they might hear of more than one gal riding sidesaddle along the streets of a town this size. Lots of gals ride handsome horses. It's a female notion, like sporting a fashionable hat. With that spooky black outfit tucked in a saddlebag, she could be pretty as a picture or fat and ugly. Canvas at this stage of the game and you're likely to wind up with a tedious list of women of every description, riding nowhere in particular, unless some old boy on his way to work chose to follow her home."

The sheriff sighed and said, "I follow your drift. Our best bet would be those horses. Three of 'em. That big black hunter and the missing stock those murdered census-takers must have been riding."

Longarm nodded, but said, "We don't know what either might have looked like. Those kids from other parts could have hired, borrowed, or been offered anything from high-stepping thoroughbreds to Spanish riding mules. To track them down, we have to come up with someone still alive who got a good look at them and feels ready to talk about it."

The sheriff suggested, "We only have to nail down *one* if the dead boys rode out on livery nags. They'd have naturally hired them from the same owner. What was that about somebody *offering* mounts to a pair of total strangers?"

Longarm explained. "Our sidesaddle assassin told Corman she didn't want them taking that census. So she must have been expecting them to try."

The Mormon sheriff nodded and said, "That works. Some two-face meeting their train and offering to outfit them with riding stock could account for a heap. Spooked ponies with suddenly empty saddles run for their cozy stalls and filled mangers on the property of their *owners* if it's not too far!"

Longarm nodded and asked, "How do you feel about separate spreads north and south of town?"

The older lawman said, "I like the notion. Say one two-face was waiting for Corman and Lescot with riding stock from one spread to the north and another to the south. Say the boys stabled the borrowed stock at the hotel and . . . Lord have mercy! I never thought to ask at their *hotel* about any riding stock they might have left out back all the time they were here!"

Longarm said soothingly, "I did. Just now when I was leaving another pony in their care. The hotel has no record of either federal employee either."

The sheriff blinked and replied, "They don't? We took it for granted they'd stay there just across from the depot."

Longarm said, "We did too. I mind that in my Army days, traveling on orders with a per-diem expense account, it was tempting to accept free room and board you could charge to your account with nobody having to be any the wiser. There's a chance they stayed at some other hotel. It's worth asking. But I'm commencing to suspect they were offered a whole lot of helpful suggestions, to set them up for the slaughter."

The local lawman grimaced and confessed, "You're starting to make me feel mighty foolish, bringing up angles I never even considered!"

Longarm said soothingly, "My boss calls it the process of eliminating. You have to practice. Where might I find this Klaus Pommer, in case he left anything out when he made his complaint?"

The sheriff said, "You can't now. That's why I had my deputies hunting high and low for you all over town. Pommer showed up not long after you'd left. He'd already sold out to his junior partner and bought a one-way ticket to Omaha. Said he was leaving on the three-fifteen. So I reckon he did, over an hour ago. Said he didn't make enough of a profit here in the Delta to worry about crazy women in spooky costumes. He'd already heard tell about those census-takers. So she scared *that* Gentile off easier."

Longarm made a wry face and muttered, "Might be a better market for bobwire at that. But what motive could she have had, and what makes you so sure she's a Saint?"

The older Mormon lawman said, "Her motives, both times, have me stumped. That government census wouldn't have slowed down statehood, and might have speeded it up. Klaus Pommer wasn't mixed up in church or political matters. As for her being a Saint, you just said she's able to ride by without attracting attention when she has to. So how many Gentile ladies on high-stepping horses do you reckon your average member of our congregation sees passing by?"

"Can you folks recognize one another as Saints at a distance?" Longarm asked.

The native of the Mormon Delta replied, "Well, the underwear we all wear may not show under modest if nondescript summer dresses, but you see, there weren't all that *many* of us coming over the South Pass with the Apostle Brigham. So our younger folk, under forty, all sort of grew up together. I'll allow a member of our Ogden congregation might not recognize a member of the Provo congregation on sight, if you'll allow the Saint in these parts would notice a total stranger on an unusual horse."

Longarm wasn't sure it would be polite to observe he had noticed a sort of family resemblance among the settlers all along the Mormon Delta. Other visitors had suggested the illusion was inspired more by national origin than any inbreeding possible in so few generations.

The Angel Moroni had inspired the prophet Joseph Smith in upstate New York as late as 1830. It had taken Smith some time to recruit his family and nearby neighbors as apostles and missionaries. Then the original congregation of Anglo-Saxon York Staters had had better luck recruiting members from *old* England than *new* England. So for reasons one likely had to be a Saint to understand, the long struggle west to what had been Mexican territory Mexico paid little attention to had been endured for the most part by immigrants from the British Isles, led by New Englanders who didn't look much different. As immigrants from other parts mixed in with the old colonial stock in *other* parts of the Union, the Mormons had commenced to look sort of different because they simply hadn't changed from the way the Pilgrim Fathers and First Families of Virginia had started out.

As long as he was on the subject, Longarm asked, "How come some of you all refer to the late Brigham Young as an apostle whilst others call him a president?"

The Mormon sheriff explained, "He was loosely referred to as our Brother Brigham because he was one of us, of course. When he first became a follower of the

Prophet Joseph, he was•naturally an apostle. When a Gentile mob lynched our first prophet and the Apostle Brigham told us this would be the place, he was acting as our prophet. But as our church is governed by a council we call the Presidency, Brother Brigham was our president, and as you know, we've only recently begun to pay any attention to a federal government we never invited out our way."

Longarm was sorry he'd asked. He didn't want to go into that so-called Mormon war that had ended in a standoff. He didn't see what shoot-outs of a generation back might have to do with a sidesaddle assassin in the here and now.

So he rose to his considerable height, explaining that he meant to lay for that mystery woman at dusk where those colored kids had spotted her jumping that ditch north of the railroad yards. The sheriff asked if he could use some help. Longarm was used to having that argument.

But this time he had a face-saving excuse for all concerned. Longarm told the older lawman, "I'd take you up on that offer, save for a secret I don't want to get around. I've borrowed a high-jumping field hunter that may match her own. There ain't many hills and dales here in your Delta, but you have a heap of fences and canals for any horse to jump. So I doubt riders mounted on more natural stock would be able to follow us far enough to matter, should I cut her trail."

He patted his holster absently and added, "If I do, I'm packing a more impressive six-gun than her bitty Harrington and Richardson .32."

The sheriff rose as well, quietly observing, "That .45-70 rifle she used on those census-takers and almost used on you this morning has a longer range and way more wallop than your Winchester saddle gun."

Longarm shrugged and said, "Rapid-fire has the edge on long-range wallop after sundown. You have to get close enough to your target to see it before you can aim any sort of gun at it. But I mean to drop her horse out from under her and discuss her surrended at some distance, lest I wind up having to shoot a woman."

As they headed out front together, the sheriff soberly asked how Longarm could get out of shooting a woman if the deadly woman in black chose to go down fighting.

To which Longarm could only reply, "I reckon I'll have to do what has to be done. I said I was anxious to avoid it. I never said toad squat about letting her get away."

# Chapter 6

The livery mount Longarm had hidden away at Camp Ogden wasn't a twin to the one he'd borrowed from Hazel Mullroony. But a paint pony was a paint pony and with any luck, anybody gossiping about him riding out of town once on a paint would report he'd ridden out of town a second time on a paint.

He got back to Hazel's shack to find she'd closed shop and rustled up an early supper for him. A gal running her own store had a swell head start on supper at any time of the day. So she sat him down at her kitchen table for fried bully-beef with canned Boston beans and pickled beets on the side, served with sourdough biscuits for sopping up, with black coffee and chocolate cake for dessert.

As they both dug in, she told him the older of the three Willard brothers would be there no later than six to show him the way to that ditch crossing before sundown. It was going on five-fifteen as Longarm pushed back from the table and asked her permission to indulge in some sinning.

She fluttered her lashes and suggested they only had

about forty-five minutes before that Willard boy came by, shyly adding she'd have told him *seven* had she known Longarm wanted to get frisky.

He managed not to laugh, not wanting to hurt any feelings, and told her he'd had lighting a forbidden after-supper smoke in mind.

She still looked hurt as she murmured, "Oh, sure, go ahead, if *that's* all you meant."

Longarm reached for a cheroot as he gallantly replied, "Oh, I'd feel frisky enough if, like you suggested, we had more time for such pleasures. But we'd best set that notion aside until I get back. If I get back, that is."

The short and chunky but purely female Hazel jumped up to come around to his side of the table and plop down in his lap as she demanded in a frightened voice, "What do you mean *if*? I don't want you to get killed tonight! Promise me you won't get killed tonight!"

He wrapped one arm around her not-too-slender but firm young waist as he assured her, "I can promise I'll *try* not to get killed, Miss Hazel. But should that mystery gal ride the same way this evening, there's just no saying how far I'll have to chase her, or how long it might take to wrap things up if I do. All us lawmen have a whole heap of questions to ask her, and even if I fail to bring her in alive, there's sure to be all sorts of papers to fill out. So even if I win, I'm likely to be busy long past your bedtime."

She snuggled closer, purring, "I'm a light sleeper. You come back here any time you want. I'm not going anywhere."

So he kissed her, didn't ask where a Paiute breed had learned to kiss so French, and never did get around to that after-supper smoke. But they kept their wits about them, and it never got past swapping spit and clutching friendly before, sure enough, there came a knock at the

47

door and she rose, flustered, to admit and introduce twelve-year-old Nero Willard.

Neither the colored boy nor the Union Pacific his daddy worked for were old enough to have suffered from the peculiar institution. So Longarm figured Nero had been named after a dad or a granddad who *had* been named by slaveholders. Longarm had never grasped the humor, or malice, inspiring the names slaves had been saddled with in the golden days of yore. Nero Willard was lucky he hadn't been handed down a handle like Beelzebub or Cadaverous. Longarm had met up with a chambermaid named Gonorrhea who'd been mercifully unaware of its meaning, and seemed pleased by the smiles she got from white folks when she told them what her name was.

Nero seemed a tad uneasy in the company of a white man Miss Hazel had identified as The Law. But they got along better after Longarm bet the kid a silver dollar he couldn't show the way to where that mystery woman had jumped the drainage ditch sidesaddle.

It wasn't far, but since Nero was afoot, Longarm led Skylark along a cinder path to the north bank of that wide ditch filled with stagnant drainage and, according to Nero, crawdads and mud puppies. He said nobody ate the mud puppies, or fat slimy salamanders, but he assured Longarm the crawdads were right tasty. Longarm had no call to argue. He'd been a boy one time. So in no time at all they were standing along a service path where cattails and some crack willow rose to screen anybody hunkered down. Longarm knew he and his tall field hunter were in sight from the far side as Nero pointed and explained there was higher ground along the far bank, between those clumps of sunflowers and ragweed. Nero said, "I can't say if that lady on the big black horse cleared a gap in them weeds ahead of time, or just knew it was there. But that's the way she come at full gallop, to cross the ditch like her horse had wings. I can show you where she and her flying horse came down, if you want."

Longarm said he did. Nero led the way on to where, sure enough, the lawman spied deep hoofprints and then some. He told the kid, "You just won another silver dollar off me, Nero. It's easy to see her big black hunter has landed more than once on this side, tearing hell out of the sod and smashing that patch of green tumbleweed flat as a welcome mat!"

As he handed the boy another silver cartwheel, the grinning Nero asked if he meant to hide out back behind those willows and reeds to await the lady's pleasure.

Longarm shook his head and said, "Not hardly. Two reasons. Me and my own puddle jumper are too big for such cover, and if she has one lick of sense she'll scout the crossing from the far side before she jumps it."

Nero shook his head and said, "She just come a-galloping the other night. Me and my kid brothers only heard hoofbeats moving fast in one direction, Cap'n."

Longarm explained, "She'd have scouted the jump first, on foot or walking her mount slow. Nobody would ever try for a blind jump wide as that if they didn't have to."

Nero demanded, "Did she come sneaking around before she made her run for it, how come she never spotted me and my kid brothers, Cap'n? We was splashing and laughing on this side until we heard someone coming at a gallop and hunkered down. How come she didn't know we were out this way if she scouted ahead like you say?"

It was a good question. Longarm decided, "She was either too damned reckless to be allowed to ride alone after sundown, or she knew you kids were there and didn't care, no offense."

Nero looked unconvinced. Longarm explained, "She's let others admire her in that mysterious hooded outfit. It wouldn't have taken much effort on her part to see you and your brothers were neither all that big nor heavily armed. How long did it take her to leap yonder ditch and tear on past you in the gathering dusk? What could you three have done to stop her if you'd wanted to?"

Nero grudgingly pointed out, "We told the law on her, didn't we?"

Longarm nodded soberly and replied, "In your own good time, after she was long gone. But you've been a big help this afternoon, Nero Willard. So you'd best get on home, and I've got some scouting to tend to while there's still enough daylight to matter."

He didn't answer when the kid asked where he meant to lay in wait for that other rider. He mounted up and reined Skylark away from the ditch as young Nero shrugged and headed home along the ditch.

Once you rode clear of the ragweed, sunflowers, tumbleweed, and such that followed the rails like hoboes, the flat range gave way to the low chaparral that belonged in the Great Basin, most of it greasewood and sage, with more wind-sewn cheat and native short grass than you usually saw where anything bigger than a jackrabbit was allowed to graze. Longarm suspected that just as most townships were inclined to, Ogden had set aside the empty lots all around to allow for future expansion of its city limits.

A few narrow paths of tamped-down soil crisscrossed the reserved range. But he found it easy enough to cut the trail left by one good-sized set of steel-shod hooves as they beelined north between clumps of chaparral. Where the meager grass hadn't been torn out by the shallow roots, he saw where galloping hooves had busted hell out of anthills, each about the size of an inverted washtub

50

and set in a wider space cleared by their busy builders, the western harvester ants who came in two breeds with about the same construction skills. The solid red ants, who bit about as gently as a wasp could sting, built bare mounds roofed with selected gravel about the size and texture of birdcage grit. The red harvesters with black tails didn't bite worth mentioning, and liked to sort of thatch their mounds with tiny slivers of dry grass. A big hoof crashing down on either made a hell of a mess, and the prints were easier to read away from the mounds, where the ants had cleared flat ground a yard or so out from their doorways. The same hooves tearing across sod where they failed to leave clear imprints were still very easy to follow. So he did until, around five furlongs from her leap across that ditch, he saw the galloping gal had ridden out on the well-traveled and unreadable post road.

Longarm reined in to confide to his mount, "This must be the place. Why don't we mosey across to the far side and wait for her as we let you graze and I sneak me a smoke out here with nobody watching?"

Skylark seemed willing enough. Longarm dismounted and tethered his field hunter on the far side of some knee-high sage. Then he lit that smoke and hunkered nearby with his Winchester across his knees, waiting for the sun to get on down.

He knew it was safe to assume a night rider following the same course of action wouldn't leave her cover in town before the light got trickier. He'd ridden a quarter hour on from where she'd be making that jump, if she meant to make another that evening. So it figured to be too dark for her to make him out on the far side as she rode out on the post road, outlined against such sky glow or starlight as there might be.

The only problem he had with the notion was what Nero Willard had said about crawdad-hunting kids whooping and splashing back yonder the last known time she'd made the jump.

Longarm knew that if *he'd* been riding sidesaddle on the dodge from the law, he'd think twice about riding the same way, especially if he suspected that he'd been spotted, once he'd taken time to consider how many other ways there might be to ride across dead-flat range on a mount that could jump most anything apt to be in the way. But when you only had one chip you bet it, and he had no better place to lay for the nasty bitch.

So he got to smoke until it started to taste like shit by the time the sun went down and then some, with nary a sound out their way but the skitter of night critters in the chaparral all about and the occasional plaintive cries of owls.

Nearby, Skylark commenced to paw and nicker in the dark as he got ever thirstier after sating himself on summer-dry grass. Longarm had an Army canteen balancing his Winchester's saddle boot on the far side. But he wasn't ready to fill the pancaked crown of his hat just yet. He told the big hunter, "Hold the thought and I'll let you water your fool self the next time we come to a ditch. Lord knows there ain't much sense in staying here much longer."

It was well after dark, with a crescent moon shedding little more light on the scene than the Milky Way spattered across the clear Utah sky behind the brighter but more scattered stars. It was commencing to look as if that other rider saw things the same way when it came to retracing one's path like a fool rabbit. *Some* folks were dumb as rabbits about that. But not too many. There was a method to that mystery gal's apparent madness, he felt sure. But she seemed to avoid repeating any pattern too closely. You couldn't count on just when or where she might turn up.

Deciding to wait her out another five minutes, Long-arm wondered some about those patterns she'd drawn for him to begin with. She'd exposed herself deliberately to issue grim warnings to at least one of those census-takers and to that bobwire peddler who'd had nothing to do with the census at all. She hadn't been bluffing. She or some-body in cahoots with her had gunned those two boys after Vince Corman had wired in her warning. So, right, she or someone she was fronting for was capable of killing in cold blood.

But in that case, why warn anybody in the first place? Why not simply drygulch anybody you had cause to put out of business and leave them to be found murdered by a person or persons unknown?

Longarm muttered out loud, "Like Mr. Barnum said, it pays to advertise. Scare enough folks by issuing death threats and following up on them and, before you know it, you have folks so scared you don't *have* to kill 'em!"

He suspected other threats the law didn't know about could account for the way no witnesses seemed willing to come forward. There was more to it than Mormon clannishness. The sheriff and his boys were paid-up Mor-mons too. So that sidesaddle assassin or some others she rode with had everybody along this stretch of the Mor-mon Delta in the dark, or too frightened to even look a lawman in the eye!

"Well, hell," he decided, getting back to his feet and moving to unether Skylark. "There's no sense waiting for a train that just ain't running this evening!"

Thanks to all that nervous smoking, he was tempted to help himself to some canteen water. But it was wrong for a rider to drink in the presence of a thirsty mount. So he mounted up and headed straighter back along the post road to water Skylark at that same drainage ditch. If it was good enough for crawdads and mud puppies, it was likely safe enough for horses.

He swilled some canteen water and rode on back to Hazel's place to assure her he was still alive. As he rode in and dismounted, he suspected she'd been listening for him in the dark. For she didn't have one candle burning as she flung open her door to sob, "Oh, Marshal, I've been so worried about you!"

He said his pals called him Custis as he dismounted closer to the door. As she came out in the dim light to wrap her tawny bare arms around him, he couldn't help noticing, as he hugged her back, she was naked as a jay.

But what the hell, he decided, as he bent to kiss her French, he'd just now assured her they were pals.

# Chapter 7

"Oh, Custis, this feels so happy!" Hazel sobbed as he entered her a second time.

Entering Hazel was easy. She was tight enough between her chunky thighs, but like many an Indian gal, she liked to squat on top and do most of the work.

Longarm didn't ask who'd taught her to screw Paiute or kiss French. She hadn't asked if he was a virgin either, and to be fair, Quill Indians didn't hold with Queen Victoria on such personal habits.

Longarm had long since learned it wasn't a matter of Indians having no notions of right or wrong. Most everybody had notions of right or wrong, but they weren't all the same, and Victorian morals struck many an Indian as scandalous. A Plains Cree who once offered Longarm the loan of a wife for the night had asked if it was true some white folks beat their own children and made others work in cotton mills. A Lakota sun dancer who'd torture you as gleefully as he was willing to torture himself might break down and bawl like a baby if you caught him in a barefaced lie. A Cheyenne horse thief who'd lift your hair and cut off your fingers for practice would starve and let his kids go to bed hungry before he'd refuse to share grub with a neighbor. It was all in the way folks were brought up, and Paiute diggers were raised to do without when they had nothing, and pleasure themselves like kids locked in a candy store when they got the chance.

So Hazel kept stuffing him with coffee and cake and stuffing herself with him to where he'd have begged for mercy if he hadn't been too proud. So he took his beating like a man and before midnight, she'd calmed down enough to share a smoke and cuddle on the corner mattress she'd been using as her lonely bed, to hear her tell.

When she asked how long she could count on his company, Longarm truthfully replied, "I can't say. How long I might want to stay and how soon I might have to go ain't up to me alone. You know why I'd like to keep folks in town in the dark about that big field hunter out in your corral, and anybody looking to shoot me in my hotel bed this evening is in for a big disappointment."

She said she could use her place, and her, for as long as he had any use for either. He kissed her moist eyelid and assured her in a respectful tone, "It ain't a matter of using or abusing, Miss Hazel. Do you want me to treat you like a child and tell you fairy tales, or would you rather have me level with you, one grown-up to another?"

She allowed most of the fairy tales white folks told sounded sort of pointless, next to the ones about Old Man Coyote or Spider Woman. So he told her, "The . . . medicine I live by doesn't allow my natural feelings to lead me astray from the trail when I'm after a killer wanted by my people. In the morning I'd like to leave Skylark here with you and mosey into town aboard your paint to ask more questions about that woman the Willard brothers saw the other night."

"When you catch her, are you going to fuck her?" the

Paiute breed asked more calmly than a pure Irish gal might have.

Longarm laughed and said, "I'm hoping I won't have to shoot her. It would be bad medicine to even kiss a gal we want to try for cold-blooded murder."

Hazel insisted, "Not even if she's pretty?"

He said, "Not even if she's beautiful." And she kissed him and grabbed hold of his flaccid manhood as she said she was glad.

So one thing led to another, and this time he got on top to hook an elbow under each chunky knee in an attempt to have some control of the situation. So a grand time was had by all, and they even caught a few hours sleep before she woke him up to serve him biscuits and bacon with his breakfast coffee, ruefully warning him she had to open for business out front and could only offer him a quick one.

He gallantly passed on the offer, lest she keep any early customer waiting, and after he'd swilled more coffee alone, he washed up as well as he was able with a basin and bucket of well water, and let his stubble go for the time being. Treating himself to a sitdown shave in town might offer the chance to pick up some gossip. Like most experienced lawmen, Longarm had found a stranger in town could pick up more gossip at a neighborhood barbershop than your average whorehouse. You were allowed to just sit still and listen in a barbershop.

After going around to the shed to say good-bye before he left, he rode into town on Hazel's paint pony. There were no messages waiting for him at his hotel. He put the paint in their stable and stored his saddle, possibles, and Winchester in his hired room. Then, first things coming first, he changed to a fresh shirt, locked up, and went to the nearest barbershop, where they were offering a shave and a haircut at the bargain price of two bits.

Entering under the tinkling bell above the door, Longarm saw that at that hour on a workday he was the only customer. So there was nothing for it but to hang his hat where he could keep an eye on it and have a seat in the one barber chair.

At the middle-aged and balding barber's suggestion, he took off his bandanna and the barber pinned the cotton-twill drape across the drape of his neck, dryly asking if he'd been taking violin lessons.

Longarm ruefully confessed he'd noticed he was overdue for a haircut, and allowed he could use a shave as well.

The barber suggested he lay back and let his bristles stew softer under a hot towel. But Longarm knew someone out their way was after him with a .45-70. So he allowed it made him proddy to have his face covered in public places.

The barber said, "Suit yourself, but don't blame me if it should feel like I'd sandpapered you. I'll tell you what, seeing you're a Gentile, I'll throw in some after-shave bay rum for two cents, all right?"

Longarm replied, "I reckon. What makes you think I'm not a Mormon?"

The barber said, "Relax, I'm a Gentile too. The name is Feldman. Aaron Feldman. They call me Airy."

Longarm said, "Pleased to meet you, Airy. What gave me away as an outsider?"

The barber said, "Like me, you're not wearing long underwear so late in the summer. You want I should lather your face or do you want we should talk about holy underwear?"

Longarm laughed and leaned back with his .44-40 in his lap under the cloth, reflecting that the bell over the door would give him a timely warning as he stared at the pressed-tin ceiling to be lathered for his shave.

As Feldman shaved him with the smooth professional speed required for such prices, Longarm reflected sheepishly on that Mormon peculiarity he'd forgotten about. The Latter-Day Saints, men and women, young and old, all wore close-fitting underwear of white cotton all the time, with square openings to expose nipples and more private parts. Unfriendly newspaper reporters and travel writers had a lot of fun speculating on Mormon orgies featuring multiple wives in long underwear. The sect seemed to draw more fire for such unusual personal habits than for any actual felonies any Mormons could be blamed for. As a man who read lots of wanted fliers, Longarm knew there were chicken thieves and worse of every religious persuasion. So while there *were* some few Mormons riding the owlhoot trail, they scored lower than average on some offenses. That travel writer Richard Burton had suggested rape and indecent exposure were rare in Salt Lake City because they were allowed to carry on in private like South Sea Island folks in long underwear. Some Mormons Longarm knew hadn't thought much of Burton's book.

The bell above the door tinkled and Longarm tensed, gun in hand, until the barber shaving him greeted the regular customer, who said he'd be back later seeing the barber was busy.

Airy Feldman said, "Suit yourself. You heard about Klaus Pommer?"

The customer Longarm couldn't see replied, "I did. The Twilight Lady ran him out of town. Miss Rachel's holding a sale over yonder, now that she'd be running the place."

The door slammed. Feldman muttered, "Everyone's in such a hurry! He couldn't wait a few minutes already?"

Wiping Longarm's face clean with a damp towel and

59

sitting him up straighter, the barber added, "So watch and tell me I cut hair too slow!"

As he began, Longarm said, "I heard something about that hardware man being spooked by somebody might odd. You call her the Twilight Lady?"

Feldman said, "*They* do. I don't call her anything because I've yet to see her or the golem. Confidential, until yesterday I thought she was as real as the golem, the Black Cossack they used to tell about in the old country, or that headless horseman Mr. Irving wrote about. But Klaus Pommer was a sensible Gentile, like me, so he must have seen something, right?"

Longarm replied, "I reckon, seeing he went out of business of a sudden. You say there's a *Rachel* running things now?"

The local barber answered, "Rachel Hall. Yankee girl from York State, like the Smith brothers. But I've never seen her underwear. So she doesn't have to be a Saint. Some say she must have been a sinner to wind up a junior partner after working for Klaus Pommer such a time. *Nu,* we live and let live. If such a pretty little thing had to bed an old goat like Pommer to be a junior partner, she *deserves* the place!"

Longarm switched the conversation back to the Twilight Lady, as some local had described that mystery rider with such difficult-to-follow habits.

Feldman was able to add one detail Longarm hadn't been told before. It seemed country tales had been told for sometime about a mysterious woman in black on a big black stallion, riding lickety-split from "Ain't Certain" to "Nowheres in Particular" around sundown. Those two census-takers and the High Dutch Klaus Pommer had been the first Gentiles she'd ever warned to leave the Delta. Feldman said he didn't know whether she'd threatened any Mormons, and confided that such country matters seemed to be settled in private. He scornfully added, "You hear so much about Saints hardly ever coveting their neighbors' wives or other livestock. *Nu,* who's to say how often they have at it like those *meshugganah goyim* Burr and Hamilton. Who'd know?"

It was a good question. Longarm didn't know the answer. As Feldman finished, they agreed outsiders sometimes had a time getting anything out of country folks who hadn't grown up next door.

Paying extra for the bay rum and smelling like a pimp, Longarm headed next for a gunsmith the barber had located for him in the the same neck of Downtown Ogden. Feldman had said Walt Beatty ran about the biggest sales and repair shop in those parts. So as Longarm found the corner shop with its display windows holding guns enough for a small war, he decided, "This must be the place."

He entered under yet another tinking bell to be greeted by the neighborly young squirt behind the back counter. Walt Beatty was about the size and build of young Henry back in Denver.

Longarm flshed his badge and identification to save time, and when he placed the spent brass from that rooftop on the glass between them, Walt Beatty went up a notch in an older gunfighter's professional opinion by picking one of the cartridges up to examine it with a jeweler's loupe and say without hesitation, "Army .45-70 fired from a bolt-action rifle. The Army Springfield has an off-center firing pin. I heard about that gunplay over to Courthouse Square yesterday. You'd be looking for a playmate packing something like the Keene bolt-action magazine rifle Remington Arms just came out with this past Christmas season."

Longarm took the brass back, saying, "Much obliged.

You sell many saddle guns of that description, Mr. Beatty?"

The young gunsmith and dealer shook his head and said, "You'd want to cut it down some for a saddle gun and I don't have any in stock. You have to order special calibers from the factory, and most Keenes are .44-70. That's already more gun than most of my Mormon customers need. The cheaper and easier-to-come-by .44-40 Winchester '73 will take down anything but a buffalo or grizzly, and you won't see many of either here in the Mormon Delta."

Longarm asked if it would be possible to rechamber, say, a more common bolt-action Chassepot. A lot of those French Army rifles had suddenly come on the secondhand market after the Franco-Prussian War.

The gunsmith, who'd have been a kid at the time, sniffed and said, "The Chassepot is a worthless waste of metal in any caliber, and not worth rechambering when there are far newer secondhand rifles to be had. I'm pretty sure you're looking for someone packing a Keene. I just don't happen to stock 'em. But where does it say a rooftop sniper couldn't have bought a bolt-action .45-70 anywhere else?"

Longarm thanked young Beatty and left, reflecing that Billy Vail's process of elimination could sure get tedious.

He asked directions, and headed next for the hardware and farm supply store abandoned the day before by that scared-off merchant Klaus Pommer.

He saw why that barber had cited gossip about the older man and his junior partner when a tall willowy blonde with a ravishing smile reached across her own counter to shake hands and invite him into their back rooms as soon as he flashed his badge and told her why he was there.

Rachel Hall looked to be pushing thirty, but was still

in fine shape under her summer-weight blue gingham skirts and tight bodice. Longarm couldn't detect the outlines of any Mormon underwear under the thin calico. But he knew they cut openings for one's nipples to squirt out of. So he was looking for square outlines *around* those inspiring features as she sat by him on a chesterfield, perched on a bentwood chair across a coffee table from him, and fluttered her lashes some as she confessed, "It's a warm day and I've been shifting lots of stock around out front."

He smiled sheepishly and replied, "I heard tell you were having a sale, Miss Rachel."

She said, "I have to. If I mean to pay my grocery bill. As desperate as he was, old Klaus knew to the penny how much I had in the bank, and I had to give it all to him before he'd sign this property over to him."

He didn't answer right off.

She flushed and snapped, "That's all he got from me. Ever. Do you think I'd have to pay any man with money if I was willing to offer my body?"

To which Longarm could only reply, "Not hardly, ma'am. You'd be able to charge a hundred a night, if that was what you were selling."

# Chapter 8

His flattery seemed to inspire her to rustle up some tea and scones. Scones were Scotch rolls that tasted better than they sounded when you smeared butter and jam on them. The barber had suspected Rachel Hall of being a Gentile from Mormon country in York State. Her accent was right for those parts, but her tea was too good for any gal who didn't have at least one Irish or English granny. When he said so, she fluttered some more and confessed to Hall being an old English name, but explained that she'd learned to brew tea from her maternal grandmother Kilgore. It sure beat all how many Irish folks had sprung from that one small island. He doubted she'd want to hear about Hazel Mullroony's Irish ancestry. So he asked about that so-called Twilight Lady scaring off her boss the day before.

Their conversation would have been shorter if she hadn't kept jumping up to serve a customer out front every time the front door tinkled. Between times, she wasn't able to tell him anything he hadn't already heard about the scare from the sheriff. She said she'd never gone along on Pommer's peddling trips along the post road, and meant to sell off the wagon and its team. When he asked if she rode her ownself, she said, "Sidesaddle. I board my Exmoor pony in the livery down by the corner. Would you care to see it?"

He said, "Ain't looking for an Exmoor pony. Looking for a black show hunter, and even if you had one, you don't work as the mystery woman who ran your boss out of town."

She smiled archly and said, "Thank you. But what makes you so sure? Haven't they told you I was a hussy out to wrap an old Dutchman around my finger?"

He honestly replied, "Yep. You should hear what they say about a federal judge and his pretty young court stenographer back at my office. It comes with such jobs, and it can get worse when you turn down an invite to the Grange dance and get called a lizzy gal."

He washed down a nibble of scone with her swell tea before he soberly explained, "You say your boss knew you well enough to charge you every dime you could afford, and I believe you. So how could any junior partner he knew that well have disguised her voice well enough at point-blank pistol range, even with a black mask or a bushel basket over her head? Your boss told the sheriff the gal who threatened him spoke educated English, and made no mention of nasal twangs or growly rasps. So, no offense, I just can't buy you as dumb enough to even try such a risky stunt. Did you say you had that peddler's wagon and its team around here somewhere, Miss Rachel?"

She said, "Out back. The carriage house opens on the alley through the block. But as I said, I mean to empty the place out for whatever I can get. I really need the money, and I don't get along with Mormon women well enough to waste time driving door-to-door along the post road."

He said, "I might be in the market for an empty carriage house in the near future, ma'am. I've been hiding out a certain mount of my own at a sort of awkward distance in case I'm right about that gal in black working out of some hidey-hole here in town. I'd be proud to put you down for a dollar a day on my traveling expenses if you'd be willing to hide my own mount out here in town."

She said that sounded fair, and asked when he'd be back with his mysterious pony. He didn't describe Skylark as he replied, "I can't say yet. Mean to ride him to the north this afternoon, and starting from where he is right now makes more sense. Have you had any offers on emptying that carriage house?"

She said, "Not at any price I'd be willing to settle for. I'm short of operating expenses. I'm not desperate. But I can move the team and wagon over to the livery at a profit, since they only charge me a dollar a week to board my Exmoor. I'll see to it this afternoon and expect you back . . . when?"

He said, "Can't say. Don't know. What if I leave five dollars with you now and we'll settle up when we know more about an uncertain future?"

She allowed that sounded more than fair. So he put the five cartwheels on the coffee table, and they rose to shake on it and part friendly. They would have parted friendlier had Longarm felt like risking a slap across his grin.

Having run out of lines to follow in town for the moment, Longarm returned to his hotel to collect his saddle and Winchester, put them aboard Hazel's paint pony, and rode back out to the shantytown before dinnertime.

Hazel joined him out back as he was transferring his saddle to the comfortably watered, foddered, and rested-up Skylark. Hazel asked if he'd eaten. He lied about stuffing his face in town because he feared he'd have coffee, cake, and mayhaps more pressed on him at more than one spread he'd be dropping by that afternoon.

Hazel looked uncomfortable and murmured, "I wanted time to explain things to you indoors. I don't want you to misunderstand, Custis. I still want to be your girl. But it might be best if we took to meeting somewhere else. There's been some . . . talk out this way."

Longarm nodded soberly and said, "I was afraid there might be. I just heard some other mean-spirited gossip about another lady in town, and I doubt she was screwing the man *she'd* been seen with some."

The Paiute breed who kept shop in a colored shanty-town sighed and said, "Most of my customers are friendly enough. But some of them seem to be Indian haters who've never gotten over my being taken in by one of their own. I could get away with sleeping with all the white men I wanted if I was one of those Gardner sisters. Nobody says a word about the three of them bedding with half a dozen white boys who work over in the yards."

Cinching the McClellan securely with a knee against the big field hunter's slate-gray rib cage, Longarm said soothingly, "I follow your drift. Me and Skylark will have to find another hideout, and if there's time I'll send word to you before I head back to Denver, and we might have us a fine old time saying *adios*."

She pouted that she hadn't wanted to say *adios* just yet. So he kissed her, even though they were outside in broad daylight, and got going before she could change their minds. It sure beat all how far from sweet the sorrow of parting could get. So a man with a lick of sense dismounted gracefully whenever he was granted such a rare opportunity.

He rode out along that same post road to where he'd waited in vain for that so-called Twilight Lady the night before. He circled to scout for sign. She hadn't ridden in off the reserved range after he'd given up. So he rode on, feeling less guilty about all that slap and tickle with Hazel Mullroony, bless her sassy bottom.

As he'd been led to expect, he commenced to see strung wire and sunflower windmills ahead as they crossed another drainage canal the easy way, on a timber-truss bridge. Breaking out a census form, he reined in at the first gate he came to. A yard dog and a gaggle of little kids barked at him until the lady of the whitewashed frame house came to her door to shout, "I'm not receiving this afternoon. The man of the house has gone to town for some hardware on sale. Why don't you come back this evening and I'll be proud to offer you some buttermilk."

He'd forgotten all about that, talking to Hazel about coffee and cake. But looking on the bright side, it was an easy way to separate Mormon suspects from Gentiles. He ticked his hat to the Mormon housewife and explained he was there to count noses for the Census Bureau.

She said, "You still can't come in. My man is not here and we've already talked to one of you census-takers. He came by here last week. Why are you still pestering us with those nosy questions?"

Longarm truthfully replied, "That other rider's mount ran off with all the papers he'd filled out, ma'am. Might you be able to describe the mount he was riding when he came by last week? We're still trying to find it."

The Mormon woman shook her head wearily and replied, "It just looked like a plain old horse to me. I wasn't paying attention. My man answered all his nosy questions while I went about my serious chores."

He thanked her, rode on, and so it went for the next four stops in a row. He was only invited in for some apple pie and buttermilk at the one place where the man of the house was home. The smallholder said he had one wife and her three sisters as adult dependents. Between them they had fourteen kids, with one of his sisters-in-law expecting.

Longarm was too polite to follow up on that admission. He made note of the 180 acres they had under cultivation, and recorded that they raised a whole lot of gray geese as well as milch goats, corn, and garden truck. The farmer bragged that his geese weeded his corn rows better than you could expect a kid to if you spanked him, and added, "Jim Bridger bet Brigham Young a dollar against every ear of corn anyone might raise out here in Deseret. It was surely a good thing for that know-it-all Gentile that we don't hold with wagering for money!"

Longarm agreed with a friendly smile, and brought up the subject of other census-takers. They established right off that somebody a lot like the late Vince Corman had been by. But as Longarm probed further, his hitherto friendly host seemed to cool some to their conversation. He claimed to disremember just when young Corman had been by, and when Longarm brought up that wire about Corman meeting up with a mystery woman some called the Twilight Lady, the man of the house said he had to get back to work and didn't know anything about any Twilight Lady. When Longarm asked if he could at least describe the mount Vince Corman had been riding, the farmer insisted it had been a long time ago, at least a week, and allowed he'd said all he had a mind to.

So it was true that at the very least they'd been sharing ominous rumors about that sidesaddle assassin's mysterious comings and goings. The only way to gather any more details would be to find somebody willing to talk who'd really seen her.

He rode on, inwardly seething at the suspicious natures of most country folks of any religion. For all their other faults, city folks got used to meeting more strangers than kith or kin. So it didn't upset them when a face they'd never seen before asked some simple question, such as which way the railroad depot might be or where you could get a good bowl of chili in that part of town. He knew that the farmer's behavior wasn't because Longarm wasn't a Mormon. Unless he exposed his own underwear or took to chanting in Hebrew or making the sign of the cross as he rode along, they had no way to tell he wasn't a Saint with a dozen wives at home and the Book of Mormon in his saddlebag. He was catching all those slack-jawed stares and evasive answers because he was a *stranger* on a country road. He'd have had little more luck getting anything out of such rustic folks if he'd been a Mormon bishop from the Salt Lake Temple as long as they'd never met up with him before.

"This is lots of fun," he confided to his borrowed feild hunter as they made their way on to the north. They got turned down cold by women alone at the next three spreads. Then the range opened some as the economics of hauling wagon loads of truck began to give way to beef and barley. A lot of romantic bullshit had been written by city slickers about the "conflict" between farm folk and cattle folk. They were often the same folk. Nobody steered a plow or roped a cow to prove his manhood unless there was something fishy about his manhood. Folks working at any chore in town or country, on land or sea, or under the ground, were out to make as much money as they could for their troubles. You raised fresh produce, milk, and eggs when you had an easy haul to the nearest market. You raised grain worth hauling slower in bulk, or made your milk into cheese and just ate your eggs, further out.

You grazed stock even further out, on less fertile soil, because you could drive it to market on its own legs, and that was what "Yippee-ti-yi-yo" was all about.

Longarm didn't know how far north he ought to push it. Judging by the luck he'd been having so far, poor Vince Corman had been forced to come back later a lot during his earlier census. There was no saying how far out he'd ridden back and forth before that so-called Twilight Lady had told him to quit and, when he hadn't, shot him in the back with that high-powered rifle.

As he thought about Corman's missing mount, with the saddlebags holding any papers he'd managed to fill out, Longarm thoughtfully asked Skylark, "How do you feel about *that* as a motive? What if somebody was worried about some questions Corman might have asked some kid or not-too-bright young sister-in-law?"

His mount couldn't answer. So Longarm replied, "That don't work so good. They killed Lescot too, and it's an open secret that heaps of folk out this way are following their old ways with both the Salt Lake Temple and Uncle Sam turning blind eyes. Has anybody asked us to make a federal arrest on charges of polygamy or sending in their tithes to Salt Lake instead of Land Management?"

Skylark didn't answer, but somebody seemed to. As Longarm cocked his head in search of the source, he made out the sounds of sincere sobbing, coming from a kid, he felt sure.

Another bridged drainage ditch lay just up the post road a piece. The sobbing seemed to be coming from the far side of some tanglewood planted along the north bank as a windbreak. As he crossed the bridge, he saw a narrower dirt lane followed the canal, just north of the windbreak, and as he reined that way he spied the source of all that heartfelt sobbing.

A nine- or ten-year-old girl in a brown velveteen riding habit and perky derby was afoot with her back to him, tugging the reins of a cordovan Morgan pony that had seen better days. As Longarm rode closer, he called out, "Ain't no use to bedevil your poor mount, sis. When they stand sawhorsed like so, they ain't going nowheres no matter how you coax them!"

The young girl turned. She was going to be a beauty any day now. But she just looked bewildered and sort of bratty as she wailed at Longarm, "She just stopped in her tracks on me and I can't even get her to follow me afoot! What was that shit you just now said about her being sawhorsed, mister?"

Longarm reined in and dismounted, ticking his hat brim respectfully to a gal too young to be talking to strange men out in the middle of nowhere, as he gravely replied, "We don't refer to what ails the poor brute as shit, sis. We call it *laminitis,* but by any name, your pony is in a whole heap of trouble!"

# Chapter 9

Longarm tethered Skylark to a canal-side cottonwood sapling as he introduced himself, making sure she understood he was the law. You had to get things straight right off with unescorted children just commencing to bud.

She introduced her sick Morgan mare as Dancer and said she was Polly Eastman from Baltimore, visiting her aunt Olivia at her Lazy H, so there, and what on earth was lemonadishness?

Longarm gently took the reins from her, patted the Morgan's jowel, and hunkered down to feel a hoof with his free hand.

It felt like Dancer had just walked across hot coals on her steel shoes. Longarm grimaced and replied, "Laminitis. Tenderness of the laminae. Think of the quick of your fingernails or toenails and consider how you'd feel if you walked on your nails and the nailbeds or quicks under all four were inflamed."

Polly Eastman said, "That's silly. Nobody walks on their fingernails!"

He insisted, "Horses do. What we think of as their feet

or hooves are oversized middle fingers and toes, with the other toes and foot bones drawn up inside what we consider their hocks. The hoof grows in a thick, well, horseshoe pattern around most of the pedal bone or fingertip, with the horny sole a sort of thick fingertip callus. Dancer's standing with her legs braced wide like so to spread the discomfort. She's discomforted as all get-out with all four hooves on fire. I suspect she's been enjoying too rich a diet and not enough exercise. You're mighty fond of her, right?"

The bewildered young rider said, "I just love her to death. Aunt Olivia gave her to me, and said she was mine forever, when I first came out here when I was seven and had no friends at all! Jason says I've been feeding her too much too. But I guess I know what to feed my own pony, and wouldn't she be fatter if she'd been eating too much?"

Longarm rose to examine the sick Morgan's teeth as he explained, "It seems to be more a matter of quality than quantity, sis. They can't say why some human folks can stuff themselves fat with sugar candy, whilst others come down with sugar diabetes on white bread. So some horses can eat themselves fat as pigs without coming down with laminitis, whilst others, as you see, were never cut out for sugar cubes or even too generous a mix of grain and grass. A horse that ain't being worked at all should eat nothing but mature grass or cured hay. A horse being worked light, say no more than an hour a day, can rate fifteen percent grain. A hardworking cow pony shouldn't be fed more than forty percent grain and sixty percent hay. Treats richer than a carrot too often ain't good for most horses. Feeding sugar cubes to a horse is as safe as feeding chocolate to a cat. It might not kill the critter right off but, as you see, it can lead to far from sweet results. We're going to have to see about getting you home some other way, sis. This poor old critter ain't about to carry you anywheres!"

She pointed east toward the mountains and said it wasn't too far to walk. He asked how far they were talking about. When she guessed at four or five miles, he said, "That's too far to walk in them boots, no offense, and how come you and Dancer were headed west if your aunt's Lazy H lies over that way?"

She stuck out her lower lip and said, "I was trying to ride her into town. I knew she's been feeling poorly and I wanted to have our vet, Doc Murtha, tell me we didn't have to shoot her. Jason said it would be best to shoot her and that can't be so!"

Longarm resisted observing that this Jason jasper was likely right. He said, "Well, I ain't fixing to shoot her and she ain't going nowheres. So we'd best ride you home double on my mount and we can talk about it along the way."

She said she didn't want to leave Dancer alone. She said she knew how it felt to be left alone. But he insisted it was the only way to get help for a mighty sick pony, and she finally let him seat her sideways atop his saddlebags, mount up from the off-side like a fool Indian, and carry her own home at a walk.

It turned out to be less than three miles, and since horses walk three miles an hour, or midways between a forced march or an easy stroll, it took less than an hour.

But that was long enough to establish along the way that her aunt Olivia was an Army widow of the Methodist persuasion. She'd been left her Lazy H, a horse-breeding spread, by an officer who'd claimed some marginal range back from the post road under the federal Homestead Act when he'd retired from Fort Douglas and promptly suffered a heart stroke. You could see how that had gone over with earlier arrivals when young Polly innocently remarked that all of their hired help were Gentiles. It seemed the crew of the Lazy H consisted of a Chinese cook, a Mexican housekeeper, four ranch hands, and their foreman, Jason Kane. Aunt Olivia's married name was Hawker. Hence the H in the Lazy H. The late Captain Hawker had likely planned on some relaxed retirement years.

Longarm didn't pursue the matter of Mormon neighbors with a kid who likely neither knew nor cared. Longarm knew that in earlier times no outsiders could have gotten away with a homestead claim in the Mormon Delta. But as in the case of the railroad center of Ogden and many a smaller flag stop across the Great Basin, the leadership aspiring to statehood had mellowed some from the tenser times of the Mountain Meadows Massacre and the Mormon War, had adopted more of a live-and-let-live attitude to outsiders, and now seemed willing to leave them be as long as they behaved themselves.

But Longarm could see how Polly Eastman might be so attached to that pony back yonder. He doubted she got invited to many neighborhood birthday parties.

When he casually asked where she went to school, young Polly said she was tutored at home by her aunt, adding that the local Mormon schools taught that the world was flat.

Longarm said he'd never attended a Mormon school or met a Mormon who'd told him the world was flat. It sure beat all how some folks felt free to invite themselves to a barn dance and request a waltz. There was plenty of unclaimed land to file on, even out here in the Great Basin, where the neighbors might not be as set in ways that might not be one's own.

Longarm became more aware of the way the young gal had her arms wrapped around his waist as they approached the tin-roofed and whitewashed sprawl she identified as the Lazy H. As they rode in, they must have been observed with interest in return.

Polly identified the taller woman who'd come out on the veranda as her aunt Olivia, the squatter woman in a Mother Hubbard as the housekeeper, and a big bearish gent wearing a white shirt, jeans, and a tied-down *buscadero* holster as their ramrod, Jason Kane. She calmly added, "I suspect he's been screwing Aunt Olivia on the sly."

Longarm didn't answer. It was none of his beeswax who might or might not be fornicating with whom, or who might be neglecting to wash Polly's mouth out with naphtha soap.

As they got within coversational range, the big ramrod stepped off the veranda to growl up at Longarm, "All right, who might you be and what have you been doing with Miss Polly?"

Longarm reined in and slid the kid behind him to the ground as he replied in a friendlier tone, "Her pony broke down near the post road. She needed a ride back. So here she is, as good as I found her. I'd be Custis Long and I've been riding for the Census Bureau."

Kane growled, "We've already talked to one of you census-takers. Much obliged and what are you waiting for, a kiss good-bye?"

The taller and prettier woman on the veranda called out, "That's enough, Jason. We're all going to go inside for some coffee now, and if the gentleman would care to sup with us in a little while, there's plenty of supper on the stove!"

Young Polly had already skipped over to the veranda to report on her misadventures. So Longarm dismounted as the burly Kane murmured, "Well, all right, but watch your manners. The lady's taken, see?"

Longarm allowed he was commencing to as he teth-

77

ered Skylark to the hitch rail in front of the main house. He added in a low tone that he hadn't come courting with a saddlebag full of census forms.

There wasn't time for Jason to answer before they joined the ladies on the veranda. Up close, Olivia Hawker née Eastman turned out to be a still-handsome light brunette in her forties who'd never had any kids of her own if he was reading those perky tits under her summer-weight bodice correctly. Polly had apparently filled her in on her sick Morgan pony by then. Once they'd how-died and sized one another up some, Olivia asked nobody in particular what they were going to do about poor Dancer.

Jason shrugged and said, "I told you your niece had killed her pony with kindness, Miss Ollie. Why don't I send a couple of the boys with a dray to put it out of its misery and salvage the hide?"

Polly wailed, "Oh, no! Dancer is my best friend! There must be some way to save her, and Mr. Long here says he knows what's ailing her!"

The Widow Hawker smiled uncertainly at Longarm, who shrugged and said, "Your foreman here would be right as rain if we were talking about the monetary value of an eight- or ten-year-old mare with a bad case of laminitis. Since we're talking about a friend, and since it's not likely to cost you any money, I'd say there was a fifty-fifty chance of saving her, or at least keeping her alive. She ain't going to be much for riding for quite a spell, if then."

Both Polly and her aunt wanted to know how he'd treat a case of laminitis. Jason snorted that there wasn't any cure. Longarm nodded and said, "He's right. There ain't. But sometimes the condition can clear up with a little help and a heap of patience."

They told him to go on. So he said, "I'd commence

by getting her back here aboard that dray. She ain't about to make it on her red-hot hooves. Then I'd pull her shoes off and turn her out to pasture on soft dry sod on her bare feet. I'd allow her all the water she might drink, but feed her nothing but the summer-kilt grass under her for as long as it takes for her condition to get better or worse on its own."

Polly protested, "That sounds cruel! Won't she get hungry?"

Longarm nodded and said, "Hungry is the natural state of a horse. Digger Indians never seem to come down with poor circulation on an uncertain diet of pine nuts and jackrabbit, either. A pony running free with nobody working it can live to a ripe old age, for a horse, without ever being shod or fed a thing but grass. You can see your pony ain't in shape to be worked. A return to the natural state of her kind might allow her to heal herself."

He locked eyes with the glaring Jason Kane and added with a tight smile, "If it don't, there'll be plenty of time to shoot and skin her. It's going to take a spell before her hooves cool off or start to peel away. Picture frostbite or the poor ciculation of, say, sugar diabetes under your own fingernails, then wait a spell to see if they get better or come unstuck."

Polly started to cry. Her aunt looked sort of green around the gills as she repeated her invite to step inside. Jason Kane swore under his breath and said he was going to see to the recovery of the broken-down mount, over by the post road.

So Longarm followed the lady of the house, her silent housekeeper, and young Polly inside. You could see right away the place had been built by an old army man. There were Indian relics and framed sepia-tones of soldiers in many monotonous poses all over the walls, which had been papered with a severe stiped pattern. The housekeeper took Longarm's hat and the Widow Hawker sat him on a love seat and perched her own shapely bottom on a foldup army field chair that might have inspired her bottom with fond memories.

Young Polly plopped her own small bottom next to his on the love seat. As the Mexican housekeeper served the three of them coffee with anise ladyfingers, seeing it was going on supper time, Longarm asked to hear more about that earlier visit by one of the murdered census-takers. The lady of the house thought a young gent she described along the lines of the late Vince Corman had been by some six or eight days back. She said she'd set him down on that very love seat and answered all sorts of foolish questions.

When she asked Longarm why on earth the Census Bureau needed to know how much land a woman who wasn't allowed to vote might have under irrigation, Longarm gravely explained, "The Census Bureau only tallies up the population in each Congressional district. They ask all those other questions for other government agencies. I reckon the Land Management office wants to know how much land is under irrigation out this way where it rains so seldom. The earlier Mormon settlers laid out all the dams and ditches of their Delta without any land management help, and somebody in Washington may feel left out. As to voting rights for landowners of your gender, ma'am, nobody has ever asked me to rule on that. If it's any comfort, women are allowed to vote and even hold public office in Wyoming Territory. I understand it was your own notion to file a homestead claim in the *Utah* Territory. Might you recall what sort of mount that earlier census-taker was riding the day he came by here? I've a serious need to know and nobody seems to be able to remember."

The widow frowned thoughtfully and decided, "That's

odd. But now that you mention it, I must not have been paying much attention. I only get a picture of a horse in general when I recall him riding in that afternoon. He was a polite young man, but some of his questions seemed annoyingly personal."

Young Polly piped up. "He was riding an old Army bay. Long in the tooth and favoring its off hind hoof. I knew it had been in the Army one time because I've seen whole parades of bays that very same color, and it still had its U.S. brand on its near shoulder, so there!"

As the two adults exchanged bemused looks, the sort of fresh-mouthed kid continued. "That other census rider rode an Army bay too. I met up with the two of them over on the outskirts of Ogden and they asked me directions, saying they were new out here. The one Aunt Olivia is talking about rode this way. The other one rode south. So there."

The widow half closed her eyes and decided, "She could be right. Living for years on Army posts leaves a sort of uniform blue when it comes to horseflesh. The sight would be fresher to a child."

Before Longarm could answer, a ranch hand he hadn't met before came in, hat in hand, to report, "Jason ain't on the spread and there's something somebody in charge should know, Miss Olivia. The Chinese just spotted something from your back porch. Says it looks like a rider on a dark horse, dressed head to toe in black and scouting us from a distance sidesaddle!"

# Chapter 10

Everyone else tore back through the house for the kitchen door. Longarm dashed out the front door to untether Skylark and fork himself into the saddle, declaring, "You've had enough beauty rest and it's time to show us what you're made of!"

He loped Skylark around the corner of the main house and across the barnyard to cut between a stable and a henhouse toward the far-off snow-flecked peaks of the Wasatch range. The sun at his back was low, but far from setting, so the mountains rose like hot coals against the cobalt-blue eastern sky, and the sage flats ahead were as well lit as some vast theatrical stage.

But he didn't see anybody else out yonder until he followed a faint column of dust that could have passed for a whirlwind down to its source, to spot a black dot farther out than he'd pictured, and moving farther out by the minute at full gallop.

So now that he'd seen for himself, Longarm knew she wasn't a local legend, and better yet, he'd caught the so-called Twilight Lady in broad daylight on dead-flat and wide-open range!

But then it got more complicated. The big field hunter under Longarm seemed willing and able to move quickly. But Longarm was a big man, and from the way that other mount was moving, its black-robed rider had to be way lighter. When a cotton bole of gunsmoke hid the distant rider for a moment, Longarm swerved Skylark to one side long before the sound of the distant gunshot followed a bullet through the space where they'd just been.

Seeing she'd fired that whore pistol, Longarm drew his Winchester from its saddle boot one-handed, and cranked a round of .44-40 into its chamber by gripping just the lever-loop and snapping the two feet of barrel and magazine tube like a whip.

As he felt his saddle gun load and lock, he fired, holding it like a pistol, and when that didn't stop the deadly distant rider, he fired again. But he decided to hold his fire when he saw his target flattened low and not looking back as she lashed her own mount with the reins. He felt no call to gun a woman when she wasn't shooting at him, and the one he was out to take alive had likely seen how dumb it was to swap .32-20 pistol rounds for .44-40 rifle rounds in a running gunfight at any range.

The hell of that was, she seemed to be slowly but surely extending the range as the heavier Longarm pursued her across the flats, noting that she'd now swerved south toward the cross-country railroad and Ogden Town. When he saw her and her black show hunter soar some through the air ahead, Longarm braced himself for the ditch before they got to it, and Skylark made the jump with little effort to land at the same dead run. Longarm saw what she was up to. Knowing darkness wasn't fixing to fall seriously for a good two hours, she was making for the drainage confusion left by running a railroad's ditches across earlier farm irrigation and then trying to repair the damage by dig-as-you-might.

So he chased her across half a dozen other ditches within the next four or five miles, and Skylark was heaving some and commencing to lather under him, although without complaint as he fought to overtake that black brute toting a lighter load. And then she jumped a really wide son of a bitch and Skylark, trying hard as he could . . . didn't make it.

"Son of a . . ." Longarm managed as Skylark's front hoof came down in stagnant water to stick in deep mud and somersault his big ass high in the sky, to spread him out across the range on the far side.

By that time, Longarm had stopped rolling ass-over-teakettle through sage and greasewood, to wind up smelling like a dusty drugstore with his breath knocked out of him.

First things coming first, he helped the shaken Skylark to his feet and made sure the gallant gray wasn't seriously hurt before he gathered up his hat and Winchester, mounted up again, and gazed off to the south in vain for some sign of that ditch-jumping bitch on—fair was fair— a damned fine lightly laden mount.

There was nothing to be seen down yonder but the spires and rooftops of Ogden. So he muttered, "Well, the game ain't over till it's over," and clucked his own jaded mount on at an easy walk.

The sun was closer to setting as he reined in at that same livery near the depot and led Skylark inside. The old livery man in bib overalls howdied him and asked what had happened to the paint they'd hired out to him.

Longarm said, "I've been riding this field hunter instead. I told you earlier I was the law. I'm still working on whether I want to arrest you on a charge of obstructing justice. It depends on how well your memory might have improved since last we spoke."

The older man blinked in surprise and protested, "I don't know what you're talking about! I haven't broken any laws! I've always been straight with all my customers! You can ask anybody here in town!"

Longarm said, "I mean to. First I want you to tell me why you told me earlier you didn't remember hiring out any horseflesh that was never returned. This afternoon I learned two murdered federal men were last seen alive on what a fairly reliable witness described as a pair of bays, wearing Army brands, one favoring an off hind hoof."

The owner of the livery nags in question brightened and said, "Oh, that sounds like our Star-Blaze and Gimpy. They ain't missing."

Longarm said, "I noticed. The other day when I was choosing that paint. My reliable witness never mentioned any white blaze. But I'd seen and rejected the broken-down cavalry mount favoring one hoof, and you have half a dozen bays in the back with Army brands."

The older man replied, "What if I do? I'm in the trade of hiring out riding stock. We all know a twenty-year-old pony can carry a rider well enough, and the Army remount service sells off any stock over eight years old at a reasonable price."

Longarm said, "I ain't accusing you of stealing Army stock. I want to know how come you said all your stock was present and accounted for when I knew for a fact that two census-takers had been shot off horses never found anywhere near their bodies. Are you trying to sell me two hired mounts returning here with empty saddles and just undressing themselves for bed without anybody noticing?"

The owner of the stock in question suggested they find

out, and yelled into the darker stable for an Alvin.

The bucktoothed kid who came forth looked neither brighter nor dumber than one needed to be to work as a stable hand. When his boss posed the same questions, Alvin shrugged and said, "I just work here. When you tell me to saddle a mount for a customer, I do so. When a customer comes back with a mount, I take charge of it and let him settle up with yourself, if there's anything to be settled. I can't name you the riders who hired Star-Blaze and Gimpy that far back. They've both been rid since, more than once."

His boss demanded, "How could two dead customers return them two Army bays, Alvin?"

The stable hand said, "Beats me. Somebody must have. The two of 'em are out in the paddock as we speak, and like I said, I recall saddling and unsaddling the pair of them more than once."

Longarm decided, "Try her this way, Alvin. Would you say you'd pay little attention to anyone getting on or off a hired mount as long as you had no occasion to converse with them?"

Alvin nodded and said, "I just did. We hire out lots of rides, at all hours to all sorts of strangers, this close to the depot."

Longarm said, "Then it's possible you might not notice if one set of customers rode out and two other riders brought the same two horses back."

It had been a statement rather than a question. But Alvin said that was about the size of it. He added with a nod at his boss that he wasn't the one who handled any money.

The owner had been thinking. Before Longarm asked, he declared, "I think we just now solved another mystery. As I was counting up our profits over the weekend, we seemed to be twenty dollars ahead, and I was sort of puzzled about that."

Longarm asked if they didn't keep written records as they hired horseflesh out. The older man looked confused. Longarm said to forget the question, adding, "Another livery owner I know told me she just wrote out a slip when one of her mounts left the premises, and discarded it once the critter was returned in good shape. So let's say the riders who returned those Army bays never asked for their deposits as they wandered off in the gathering dusk."

He turned back to Alvin to ask, "Is it safe to say those two bays were returned around sundown, possibly by the same rider?"

Alvin protested, "How should I know? I saddle and unsaddle the same damned horses at all hours, day after day, and you're asking me about last week? Just tell me which way works best for you and I'll be proud to swear to it in court if I have to."

Longarm smiled thinly and allowed Alvin had given him enough for now, adding, "It sure beats all how simple the answers to some real posers can turn out, once you consider them from a dumber angle. I had them missing mounts driven off to some Ali Baba cave by them forty thieves when, all the time, they weren't missing at all. This stage magician gal I used to know calls such flimflammery misdirecting. The mysterious night rider we're after seems to have heard of it. I hate it when owlhoot riders do that!"

The livery owner asked if he'd like them to rub his lathered mount down, water him, and offer him a manger of seed hay with some alfalfa pellets thrown in.

Longarm shook his head and said he had other plans for Skylark that evening. When the older livery man suggested the lathered field hunter was about spent for the day, Longarm said, "I noticed. I don't mean to ride him hard or far. You're still holding my deposit for that paint I hired off you earlier. So I'll be on my way, and I thank you both for helping me clear up that simple bit of stage magic."

Neither argued as he led Skylark back outside and mounted up. He rode over to the Western Union to send a message to Billy Vail, more to give the sun more time to set than for anything more than a simple progress report sent at night-letter rates.

Then, remounting in the tricky light of a Great Basin sunset, he rode over to the hardware now owned by Rachel Hall. As they passed, he saw she'd lit lamps inside to wait on some customer. So he rode around to the far side of the block and along the alley to the rear of her property, where he found the big alley doors of her carriage house unlocked when he dismounted.

There was enough light left to see she'd emptied the place out for them. He led Skylark inside, put him in one of the two stalls, and unsaddled him to rub him down with some handy gunnysacking. He smiled fondly when he found the drinking trough already filled with fresh water and the manger filled with coarse mixed oats and chopped hay. High-quality timothy hay, from the smell of it. You had to admire such a gracious hostess.

He saw the alley doors could be bolted from the inside. So, seeing his saddle and Winchester would be as safe or safer there than in his hired room at the hotel, he ducked out the smaller side door into her backyard, took a leak in her outhouse while he had the opportunity, and moseyed over to her back door.

It wasn't locked. He hadn't expected it to be, since she'd doubtless been expecting his company. He stepped inside without knocking to find himself first in a kitchen and then that same back room they'd talked in earlier.

He peered out through the curtains to see Rachel Hall closing the front door after her departing customer. So, as she turned around, he stepped out to howdy her.

The tall willowy blonde gave out a startled gleep, and staggered back a step before she recovered to say with a relieved smile, "Oh, it's you! Do you always pop out like a jack-in-the box, Custis?"

He said, "Sorry. I forget how quiet I walk in these low-heeled Army boots, Miss Rachel. I just took the libery of stabling a mighty tired steed out back. I hope that's jake with you?"

She said she'd moved her own team out with that in mind, adding, "I've found a buyer for the peddler's wagon. They offered to sell the team on commission for the best price offered. Have you had your supper yet?"

When he confessed he'd been too busy, she asked him to lock the front dooor for the night while she doused the lamps out front. He'd thought he'd smelled something good on his way through her kitchen. She sat him at the pine table and dished out the lamb stew she'd been simmering on the stove, serving it with cooled-off soda biscuits for sopping and reheated coffee to wash it down, as he brought her up to date on his busy afternoon.

She said he sure led an eventful life, and asked if he felt safe at his hotel, seeing the Twilight Lady had gotten away after she'd already tried for him in town earlier.

Longarm grimaced and replied, "It gets worse when you consider how tough it would have been for a woman to return a livery nag hired out to a man. Twice."

Rachel stared wide-eyed and asked, "Do you suspect she has male confederates?"

He shrugged and said, "At least one. Same cuss

could have made two trips as she held some reins on the outskirts of town. But even one pair of pants makes one wonder. Why would any gal with a man or more to back her play want to show herself sidesaddle to begin with?"

Rachel said, "Have you considered a man riding sidesaddle in a dress?"

Longarm said, "Sure I have. But two men she threatened recalled her as sounding female, and I just this afternoon established she can't weigh more than the average gal. But that don't mean she can't be scouting or fronting for a killer of the male persuasion. A gal who prefers to wave a bitty .32 Harrington and Richardson might find your average .45-70 rifle cumbersome. So I confess I do have some reservations about bedding down for the night at a known address."

She said, "I moved my own belongings here this afternoon, seeing Klaus Pommer sold his comfortably furnished quarters to me as well and the rent's almost due on the place I've been staying. So I've plenty of room upstairs and you'd be welcome to stay the night, as long as we can get one thing straight first."

He nodded easily and said, "I generally stay put when I agree to bed down on a sofa, Miss Rachel."

She said, "That's not what I wanted to get straight with you. I've a reputation to consider, and it's not true I was sleeping with Klaus Pommer, no matter what you've heard."

"Separate quarters would have made no sense if you'd been sleeping together," Longarm agreed.

She flushed, and looked away to murmur, "Don't be crude. I know we're both adults of some experience, and Lord knows it's been a while, for me at least. But if I let you sleep with me upstairs, you have to promise not to talk nasty, ask me to take it up my ass, or tell a living soul about it, ever!"

Longarm quietly observed only kids kissed and told. So she cut him some peach cobbler for dessert before she led him upstairs for some sweeter delights.

# Chapter 11

Another consideration that kept Longarm single was how different women could get without anyone having to be ugly. In contrast to the short, dark, and chunky Hazel the night before, the tall, blond, and willowy Rachel, like a lot of white gals, wanted to be on the bottom, in the dark, with her sateen nightgown on.

She seemed to find his lovemaking a whole new experience too, as soon as he had her jay naked with her bedlamp aglow, and on the bottom in deference to her expressed desire.

She seemed to enjoy his enthusiasm, inspired by the totally novel view as he long-dicked her on locked elbows with her more slender fundamentals atop two pillows and her long shapely legs thrown wide to the winds of desire. She sobbed for him to cut that out; then she laughed like hell as his love-slicked shaft kept making farty noises on the downstrokes. Then she told him not to stop, not to ever stop, as she blushed in embarrassment and climaxed hard enough to squirt a man out if he hadn't known enough to leave it all the way up inside her as he felt her innards trying to immitate a milkmaid's soft but determined grip.

Thanks to his having survived Indian torture the night before, he wasn't able to come in her without moving. So as her contractions calmed down some, he commenced to satisfy himself, and as he did so, Rachel sobbed, "Oh, my lands! Are you trying to come again? Do you really find me that desirable, darling?"

To which he could only reply, "I'm still at it, ain't I? Would I be working this hard if I wasn't enjoying you a heap?"

She sobbed that that was one of the most romantic things any man had ever said to her, and commenced to prove it by biting down with her innards again as she commenced to combine the hip movements of an Arab belly dance with a South Sea Islands hula hula. So the next time she came, he was right there with her. He felt it all the way down to his curled-under toes, and since she'd taken to calling him her darling, he felt it only polite to address her as honey instead of Miss Rachel.

He did so, as they shared a second-wind smoke. Being she wasn't a Mormon and they were not in public, Rachel confessed she'd often wondered about smoking a wicked-looking cheroot, and added she feared he was leading her far astray from her prim and proper upbringing in York State.

Such observations naturally led to the exchange of life stories that tended to go with such talk. Hers was another version of the one about losing one's cherry to a small-town minister whose wife hadn't understood him, leaving town under a cloud with a taste for adventure, and knocking around to learn ever more about men and money, with making money easier to learn.

Like many a man of action who'd talked some after the action, Longarm had learned to talk less and less about his past. It wasn't that he had all that much to hide. It was simply because it sounded more and more like bullshit to gals who'd never ridden in a war or shot it out with anyone unless you explained a lot, and then explained about your explanations to the point of tedium. So when it came his turn to dwell on the past, he changed the subject to the then and there.

He explained, "A lawman has to learn not to play chess when the name of the game is checkers. Most honest folks are way smarter than most crooks, and that can give the crooks an edge on us."

She protested that sounded silly, and asked why nobody had been able to catch that mysterious Twilight Lady if she was so dumb.

He said, "I just told you. Have you ever mislaid a set of keys and hunted high and low for them in vain, wondering where they could have run off to?"

She snuggled closer and declared most everyone had. So Longarm went on. "Same deal. Them keys or, say, the pocket comb you were sure you'd left in the same pocket don't have to be *smart* to hide themselves from you. You just have to keep looking for them in all the wrong places. I just told you about all the brain power we've wasted on those mysteriously vanishing livery nags. It's hard to see why, now that it's clear the killer or killers just helped themselves to the census riders' personal saddlebags and returned the hired nags and livery saddles to an uncaring Mormon stable boy. I'm convinced that once we know that sidesaddle assassin's motive, it's going to turn out simple as pie."

Rachel asked, "What if she doesn't have a motive? What if she's just crazy? I can see why some Mormon fanatic might want to prevent a government census. But why would she or her cult want to drive old Klaus out of the territory?"

Longarm said, "Ain't sure she's a Mormon, or trying to prevent the census itself. The Salt Lake Temple wants statehood, and come election time this fall, if push comes to shove, they'll be able to prove a fair enough head count of each township from the tithes they collect from each and every Latter-Day Saint."

Being from other parts, she didn't follow his drift. Longarm told her, "All the Saints volunteer a tithe, or ten percent of their yearly profits, to the central temple in Salt Lake City. So if they had to, the Mormon majority could provide notorized rolls of family heads, family holdings, and doubtless answers to questions no Saint would answer for a Gentile census-taker. As for your recent boss, he drove up and down the Delta in that wagon you just sold. Talking to all sorts of folks about their spreads, their needs, and who knows what else. That what else my be the question before the house. I doubt the Twilight Lady or anybody backing her is worried about raw figures. Finding out how many Mormon families there might be in this Delta would be simple, more ways than one, and impossible for anyone to prevent. So what might outsiders, taking a census or selling hardware, stumble upon out yonder without knowing they were looking for it?"

The naked lady in his arms repressed a shudder and replied in a concerned tone, "I've no idea! Klaus never mentioned anything suspicious about any of his clients to me. Do you think I have anything to worry about now that I've taken his place here?"

Longarm kissed the part of her hair and said soothingly, "You ain't taken his place. He was outside town in that wagon when the spooky gal in black warned him he wasn't welcome there. You said yourself you felt uneasy out yonder and meant to give up the door-to-door parts of the business. If *I* know that, the ones who wanted Klaus Pommer out of the territory know that. So they'd be dumb to chase you out now. If they did, you'd doubtless sell the business to yet a third party, and they'd be chancing an unknown quality buying another wagon to take up where poor old Pommer left off, see?"

She replied by taking the cheroot from him to snuff out so they could kiss more seriously. So, having gotten his second wind by then, Longarm didn't feel like jawing about Twilight Ladies' motives as he responded to Rachel's, which were easier by far to fathom, with her on top this time.

A willowy white gal with her blond hair down and thrashing back and forth across her bounding bare tits didn't look anything like a chunky Paiute breed in the same position, although closing his eyes to picture first one and then the other bouncing up and down his old organ-grinder could surely snap it to attention.

He'd learned more than once, the hard way, that bedding two gals in one's mind had advantages over really going to bed with two real ones. He didn't have to worry about Hazel and Rachel fighting over him or, even worse, deciding that as long as they were exploring new notions, they'd just ignore him for a spell as they tried out some slap and tickle they'd often wondered about. For imagining the two of them in turn with his eyes shut, he didn't even have to introduce the oddly matched but equally passionate bedmates as he enjoyed a couple of strokes in one and a good hard stroke up the other until, as they both climaxed with Rachel's longer and leaner torso against his, he remembered Hazel sucked tongue a lot different, and then shot all he'd been holding back into good old Rachel.

After that they got some sleep, but she let him show her the cold gray dawn delights of dog style before they enjoyed a cold shower together and a sitdown breakfast of waffles and fried sausages at her kitchen table.

As she served him, Rachel giggled and allowed it

made her feel as if they were living together.

Longarm wasn't certain he wanted either of them to feel like that. But he knew it was the wrong time to remind her he was a tumbleweed passing through on a field mission that would end the minute he had things wrapped.

Meanwhile, he didn't. She offered a better hideout than the more complicated Hazel, and if that made him a dirty dog to either of them, so be it. Was it his fault that men and women both deserved something better than one another?

Like many a man before him, Longarm had been played for a sap or used as a port in a storm often enough to know you just never could tell. For we all came into this world with the only person we really knew locked inside our skulls, and went out of it never having really shared one thought, for certain, with another. He'd sometimes suspected this sure and certain uncertainty drove a lot of folks to wild attempts at total intimacy that were forever doomed to failure. So he'd learned to take gals at their word until he caught them breaking it, and just loved 'em and left 'em on the level with a clear conscience, having never lied more than he had to or beaten any gal with a big black whip.

After hurrying her own breakfast coffee, Rachel said she had to open for business if she meant to stay in business. So they kissed and parted friendly, with Longarm headed over to the sheriff's department and then the federal building to leave word about the simple answer to those mysterious livery mounts. He got both places early enough to avoid tedious sit-downs with either county or federal management.

Dropping by his hotel on foot to see if there were any messages before he went to the Western Union, Longarm found a hand-delivered message from a Lawyer Vogel who said it was both important and most delicate if Longarm would care to drop by his office across from the depot.

Longarm did—it was only a short walk—to find Lawyer Vogel had a mighty handsome secretary who told him to call her Lilo. Lawyer Vogel said his friends called him Frank, instead of Franz Josef. He'd arrived in the States in '48 as a kid, and been raised the rest of the way as a Yankee Doodle Dandy to become a member of the National Grange and the American Bar Association.

Lawyer Vogel still reminded Longarm of Chancellor Otto von Bismarck at the age of forty, but without the spiked helmet and dressed in a summer suit of pongee the color of autumn leaves.

Vogel sat him down and offered him a four-bit cigar from the box on his acre or so of genuine mahogany desk, while bragging that his daddy had been a *von* in the old country, but that *he* believed in the rule of the people. Longarm accepted the smoke as politely as the seat, but asked if Vogel had been pals with Klaus Pommer, since they both seemed to hail from the same old country.

Lawyer Vogel leaned forward to confide, "That's one of the things I wanted to talk to you about. Klaus Pommer was well respected among those of us you might consider German-speaking Gentile raisins in a Mormon loaf of raisin cake. We've an election coming up in November, and while it's hopeless to think of winning anywhere else in the Utah Territory, it would be nice to control this one township where we *are* in the majority."

Longarm got his fancy cigar going before he shrugged and told the small-town politico, "Local politics are none of my beeswax. Since you seem to know so much about me, you ought to know I've no call to take sides in such matters."

Lawyer Vogel laughed easily and said, "I'm not trying to recruit you as a campaign worker. I'm suggesting some motives for this Mormon skullduggery! We *were* counting on Klaus Pommer to help get out the German-American vote for us this fall. As you probably know, most of those immigrants who fled Bismarck's Pan-Germanic Reich after the failure of the Republican Revolution of '48 joined the American Republican Party, without thinking, on arrival here."

Longarm said, "No, they didn't, no offense. There wasn't no Republican Party before they formed in the late fifties to elect Abe Lincoln. I was invited to the war that resulted. So I know."

Lawyer Vogel grimaced and said, "Whatever. The point is that neither the national Republican nor Democrat machines seem to feel there's enough political hay to be made in the Utah Territory to mount serious campaigns. So our local chapter of the Grange has to carry the torch by default. While it's true most of the Gentiles in this county usually vote Republican or Democrat, we've been trying with some success to get them to vote a straight Granger ticket come November."

Longarm asked how that might effect the price of eggs in China or the case he was working on.

Lawyer Vogel asked, "Isn't it obvious? First they murder those two census-takers. Then they run off one of the most influential Gentile merchants! The Mormon machine isn't about the lose control of even this one county. But to stuff the ballot boxes in the fall they want to keep the population figures fuzzy!"

Longarm blew a thoughtful smoke ring and said, "You ain't the first local Gentile to suggest that notion. The Salt Lake Temple's tithe recordings would prove or disprove any challenged election returns come November."

The Gentile politico snorted, "You believe the powers

that be in the Utah Territory would expose ballot box stuffers of their own persuasion?"

Longarm said, "Yep. So far the Salt Lake Temple's been straight with me. They sent me out this way on this case because I've had to arrest my share of unsaintly Saints, and I've never had much trouble on the job from what you might call the Mainstream Mormons."

He blew another thoughtful ring and added, "So tell me this and tell me true, ah, Frank. How would we ever check up on your own Granger votes, come November, if the figures were challenged?"

Lawyer Vogel stared owl-eyed and gasped, "*Zum Teufel!* Are you suggesting *my* party could be out to stuff the ballot boxes this November?"

Longarm easily replied, "Why not? You just now suggested the Church of Jesus Christ of Latter-Day Saints was out to, and like I said, the Salt Lake Temple records the church tithes of each and every tithe-paying Saint. So might the National Grange keep records of Republicans or Democrats who might or might not vote the Granger ticket, come the fall elections out this way?"

# Chapter 12

When glaring like an outraged Prussian officer didn't seem to be working, Lawyer Vogel grinned sheepishly and said, "I can see why they sent you out here to sort this can of worms. You're sharp as well as impartial. I like that in a lawman unless I'm on the defense team. But to answer your logical question, almost all the farm and stock-spread families surrounding Ogden are Mormons, as you might expect. To gain political control of a county where Gentiles are in fact the majority, we have to get all the Gentiles to vote as a block for a change. Since ballots are secret, you don't have to register as a Granger to vote the fine Granger slate we mean to put up this time. But you do have to register, and instead of sending to far-off Salt Lake City for the population figures of Ogden Township, you only need to consult the local directory on file with the Ogden Chamber of Commerce just down the street, or if you'd rather, the county clerk, who's a Mormon, naturally."

Longarm blew another smoke ring silently.

Lawyer Vogel said, "I'll bite. How would you go about getting a Gentile chamber of commerce and a Mormon county clerk to fiddle with the figures in separate files?"

Longarm said, "I'm working on it. Heve you ever tried to put a jigsaw puzzle together with a whole lot of pieces missing? I can't make any sensible pattern out of what I have so far. So I reckon I'll be getting it on down the road to see what else I can find out."

They both rose, shook on it, and parted friendly enough, with the politico yelling mean things about Mormons after Longarm.

Longarm could have yelled things back about the infamous and unconstitutional "Extermination Order" signed by Governor Lilburn Boggs of Missouri, or the lynchings of the Prophet Joseph and his brother by that mob at Carthage, Illinois, in '44. Fair was fair, and Longarm knew that had *he* traipsed clean over the Great Divide on foot, pushing all he owned in a handcart into parts not yet claimed by a country that had no use for him, he might feel a tad resentful when that country followed him over the South Pass and told him his own ways were wrong.

But Longarm hadn't been there and had no dog in that fight. So he wired another progress report, and strolled up the alley behind the hardware to slip out of town aboard Skylark some more.

After such a swell night with Rachel, he felt no call to drop by Hazel's shed, and she'd asked him not to anyhow. So he rode out past that crossroad where he'd met up with young Polly and her sick pony. Then he rode on further, consulting the survey map from a saddlebag for the county line. Like most counties, this one ran thirty by thirty miles, allowing every county resident no more than a fifteen-mile ride or wagon drive into the county seat in case they had business around Courthouse Square. Fifteen miles at the most made for half a day's ride in and supper time at home if you didn't shop too hard, or a fair haul to town for a heavy load of produce. So that was how come there were fewer produce farms and more grain and grazing as he rode ever closer to the county line north of town.

The cows he met along the way were mostly fawn-colored and sort of dangerous Jerseys, the wilder but less-apt-to-charge-you Spanish longhorns, or an unpredictable mixture of the two. The Saints had come out from the East with a few draft oxen and dairy stock being herded on foot. Bigger beef herds from down Mexico way had come north in greater numbers since Captain Cameron of the Texas Rangers had come home from the Mexican War with war trophies on the hoof that could muster and breed on marginal range and little water. Longarm hated it when you mixed fast-moving beef stock with naturally meaner dairy stock. This Mexican bullfighter he knew had confessed without shame that he'd face two Spanish fighting bulls and a rhinoceros in the same ring before he'd tangle with a Jersey bull. Jersey cows were almost as bad. It was a simple fact of nature that more men had been killed by Jersey dairy cows than all the other breeds combined, and *no* dairy cow was a pussycat.

But none of the stock he passed that day seemed to be spoiling for a fight. There was always water within easy distance and the grazing was good on the Mormon Delta, thanks to the need for all those drainage ditches. As he approached a windmill spinning in the middle distance, Longarm reflected on the healthy water situation on most spreads out this way. Nobody with a lick of sense drank ditch water, and irrigation by gravity alone got needlessly complicated in the new machine age. So, seeing the main dams and channels had the underground water table within easy reach out here on the Delta, most spreads now pumped clean sand-filtered water for their households, watering stock, or irrigation by way of smaller shallow ditches draining into the network of bigger canals. A lot of the cherry trees they'd been planting out this way didn't need to be watered, once they'd sunk their roots some. It was enough to make a Colorado rider jealous. For unlike the wild chokecherries of the High Plains, whose roots had to go down considerably, the cherry trees of the Utah Territory were real no-bullshit *eating* cherries, sweet enough to eat raw with no sugar on 'em!

As he got closer he saw that the spread ahead, like the Lazy H, lay back from the post road a ways, though not as far. Their whole section of range was fenced with bobwire. Their own wagon trace off the road led through the wire across a cattle guard of cottonwood logs laid three or more inches apart. Had he been riding a cow pony, he'd have dismounted to lead it across the deliberately treacherous footing. Skylark just jumped the six foot of cattle guard as if it wasn't there.

He rode on to yet another complex of whitewashed frame siding and tin roofing.

As he reined in out front, an older man wearing chinked chaps and a Greener Ten Gauge came out to greet him with a polite but firm request he state his name and business there.

When Longarm explained who he was and why he had to rerun the census, the stockman nodded in an approving way and declared, "We heard about you. You're the one who cured that little Gentile girl's pony, over to the Lazy H."

Longarm laughed lightly and said, "That's the trouble with word of mouth. Bust a jar of olives on the walk and by the time your story travels a mile, a wagon load of watermelons got hit by a railroad train. All I could do for little Miss Polly over yonder was identify the cause and *suggest* a cure. I fear her overfed and over-the-hill

Morgan is a long way from cured. But with any luck she may live until Miss Polly gets attached to another pet."

The shotgun-toting Saint said, "Get down and come on inside anyway. After you have some buttermilk and a slice or so of cherry pie, I got a good old mule you might like to take a look at."

Longarm dismounted, protesting he wasn't any infernal vet. But when the older man said his critter seemed to be getting worse by the day, and described the symptoms, Longarm muttered, "Sounds like the heaves. Can't promise anything, but I'd best have a look before I have any buttermilk. It's distracting to sit at a table and worry about what's going on in a barn. You have been keeping your sick mule in a barn, right?"

As Longarm tethered Skylark, a motherly woman came to their door to stare out, worried. Her man called, "It's all right, Moll. This is the horse-doctoring census-taker we heard about. We're going to have a look at old Lilburn."

As the Saint led the way around the house, Longarm didn't ask why a Mormon stockman might have named a jackass after a governor of Missouri. He said, "You see the heaves more in Denver, where I spend some time, than outside of town, where stock ain't kept indoors as much. It sure is a caution how easy it is to kill any member of the equine clan with kindness."

As they approached the big hip-roofed barn, the worried owner of the ailing jackass said, "Don't ride old Lilburn anywheres. He hauls our buckboard into town now and again. Haven't worked him hard since quite a while. Haven't needed to. Got things settled in here, as you can see. So I reckon old Lilburn's been having it too easy, like you said about that little Gentile girl's pony. But I know better than to feed cracked corn to a mule that's not being worked much. Lilburn hasn't been having anything but hay from the loft above and the same water the rest of us drink."

Longarm said, "I don't doubt it. If my suspicions are right, you may have quite a haying chore ahead of you all."

In his stall under the half-filled loft above, Longarm found poor old Lilburn, a no-longer-young but once-handsome Missouri mule, in mighty poor shape.

Lilburn was having too much trouble breathing to notice anything else as Longarm led him outside to examine him in the sunlight. The critter stood head down with strings of snot dangling from its muzzle, and most telling of all, a sweaty "heave line" crisscrossed its belly where the diaphragm had been taxed to cough air out its clogged nostrils. Like horses, mules could only breathe in and out through their noses. They couldn't breathe through their mouths worth mentioning. So a stuffy nose that would hardly keep a kid home from school would kill a big strapping draft horse.

Longarm said, "It's a wonder you've only got this one critter down with the heaves. I take it you've been feeding your other stock more grain and letting them graze outside?"

When the older man agreed that was the way you ran a stock spread in high summer, Longarm said, "You'll want to empty out your hayloft and burn every last stem. Make sure you don't leave any scattered around. Then you want to wash out yonder barn, top to bottom, with first lye water and then brine. Then you want to let it dry out, all the way, before you cut fresh hay for the winter, and this time, make dead certain it's been sun-cured right before you loft it, hear?"

The owner of all that now-worthless fodder blanched and demanded, "Are you saying there might be something wrong with the hay on hand?"

Longarm said, "Ain't any might about it. Just listen to this witness. Old Lilburn's been poisoned by spoiled hay. There's this fungus that thrives on improperly cured hay in dark lofts. Once its spores get in a hay-fed critter's lungs, more fungus sprouts in the lungs. Don't grow as well in there. But it grows enough to inspire one hell of a heap of snot to heave up."

"Is there any cure? Is he fixing to die?" asked the owner of the heaving jackass.

Longarm said, "We've been having fine sunny weather for a spell. If you turn him out to pasture on clean grass and water the sun's been shining on, he may or may not recover. I'd say it's sixty to forty in his favor, seeing he's a mule. A horse his age would have died of the heaves by this time. Like I said, you see it a heap in Denver, where too many carriage horses are stabled in too many musty brick stables and folks buy hay in bulk and store it indefinitely."

The older man bellowed, and when some boys in their teens ran out of the house to see why, he told them what had to be done while he invited their honored guest in to sit a spell.

So they got to work as Longarm followed his host into the kitchen for that promised buttermilk and cherry pie. Both tasted swell after so much time in the saddle. But he had to consider the mount he'd been riding, and said so.

The man of the house ducked out to shout more orders to his hands, his kids, or whatever, as the lady of the house cut him another slice of cherry pie.

So Longarm settled down and, sure enough, he established that they were Moll and Elisha Russell, and they got along well enough with Gentile neighbors to have heard about his earlier first aid for that other ailing critter. When Longarm said that reminded him of what he'd

107

come to ask them about, and asked how many Gentile neighbors they had, old Elisha said, "Just a tolerable few. Our kind has ever been ready to meet Gentiles partway. How would our missionary work proceed if we threw bricks at strangers who weren't throwing bricks at us? We Saints seem to be outnumbered over in Ogden Town, and they sell tobacco, coffee, tea, and worse in Ogden openly these days. But of course, out *this* way *we* get to call the tune if anyone wants to dance with us."

Longarm asked, "What happens to outsiders who don't want to dance to your tunes, Brother Elisha?"

The older man shrugged and said, "We turn our backs on them and if they don't like it, they can settle somewhere else. I know you've heard stories about the Danite riders, a generation past and never as bad as you Gentiles have been told. Too many reporters from the outside world seem to confuse elders, who may have carried things a little far, with that Moslem Old Man of the Mountains and his fanatic assassins back in ancient times."

Longarm had been raised to respect his elders. So he didn't see fit to remark that the Persian Assassin Cult was still said to be at it in the Middle East, or that he'd tangled more than once, up close and fast-draw, with more than one Danite fanatic left over from ancient times and riding for elders the Salt Lake Temple might not approve of and vice versa.

He observed instead, "*Somebody* seems to be playing assassin here in the Delta. Sidesaddle. Dressed in a hooded black riding habit aboard a black show hunter. I don't suppose you'd know anything about that, Brother Elisha?"

The man of the house said, "Well, sure I would. You're talking about the Twilight Lady. We've all known all about the Twilight Lady for many a year. They say she started riding along the skylines just at sundown since . . . How long's it been, Moll?"

His motherly wife, apparently his only one, shrugged and decided, "Oh, land's sake, a good dozen years or so. Wasn't our poor president Young still alive when we first started hearing about her spooky ways, dear?"

Her husaband said, "He was. Some say the Twilight Lady escaped from his harem to ride the range seeking revenge on depraved Mormons who kidnap Gentile maidens. Others relate her to Will-o'-the-Wisp, or Jack-O'-Lantern."

Longarm said, "Hold on. No offense, but she's been seen by at least three witnesses, including me."

The man who hailed from those parts shrugged and said, "Over to Ogden Town, little Gentile kids see Santa Claus kids every Christmas shopping season in Kruger's toy shop. That's not saying there's really any Santa Claus, and I have my doubts about the Tooth Fairy."

# Chapter 13

Longarm declared, "All right. Let's say anybody can dress up like Santa Claus or any other folk myth. Are you saying none of your own kind have ever been harmed or even threatened by that mysterious woman in black?"

The elderly Saints both nodded. The motherly Moll said, "She's just a made-up haunt invented by some kids, likely Gentile kids just passing through on their way to Virginia City or San Francisco. We don't follow those Irish Halloween notions."

Longarm nodded soberly and said, "I noticed that when I was in Salt Lake City around that time of the year. But if that sidesaddle spook hasn't got the Indian sign on you and your own kind, how come it's so tough to run a federal census out this way? The late Vince Corman wired he was having lots of trouble *before* he was told to give it up as an unwelcome chore, and I haven't had much better luck getting some of your neighbors to talk to me."

Elisha Russell sighed and said, "How much luck do you reckon a visiting Englishman might have in an Irish

Catholic neighborhood, or a Russian Orthodox official asking personal questions of Jewish immigrants chased out of Russia by those Cossack riders? Time heals, and our grandchildren won't have personal memories of burning homes and temples against eastern skies behind them. But there are still all too many among us with bitter personal memories of a government that failed to protect them and used the very words of our leaders to brand us as outlaws. Why do you find it so hard to see why many of us would as soon hold our tongues around anyone riding for the U.S. Government?"

Longarm smiled thinly and said, "Spoken like the late Chief Crazy Horse, and let's concede he had a point. But didn't anybody explain it's in the interest of all the voters out this way to let the government take a true and impartial census before the next election?"

Elisha Russell nodded and said, "That census-taker you mentioned earlier did. He was out here the day before they say he was shot in the back. Moll and me answered his first questions. But he was a brassy kid with a knowing smirk, and when he got to where we heeded our calls to nature, I told him the interview was over! I mean, why on earth would the federal government want to know how many outhouses we might have on our own property?"

Longarm explained, "I suspect the Commerce Department wants to know how the sales of indoor plumbing fixtures are coming along. A government surveyor named Powell, John Wesley Powell, seems mighty concerned with how much water it's going to take to settle all this semi-arid western range. I'm sorry if young Vince felt awkward about such questions and grinned nervously. I won't ask it, since you find the question too personal."

Elisha Russell said, "Well, since you've asked polite, we keep two crappers going at a time. One just out back

111

and another by the bunkhouse. We naturally dig a fresh pit and shift 'em every six weeks or so. I understand that Gentile Widow Hawker has indoor plumbing in her main house and a regular two-holer out behind her own bunkhouse."

Longarm didn't ask how they knew. Hired help from different spreads met in town, and that young sass Polly Eastman had a free way of talking about her elders.

Politely declining another slice of cherry pie, Longarm thanked the Russells and allowed he had to get it on down the road. So old Elisha yelled out the back, and one of his young hands brought Skylark around to the front, the horse looking as if he'd just had some buttermilk and cherry pie his ownself.

Knowing he hadn't, Longarm decided to call it a day, now that he had a better handle on local reluctance to talk to strangers. As in the simple solution to that mystery about those livery mounts, the one about the woman who'd threatened Vince Corman and Klaus Pommer was shaping up more like checkers than chess. The mystery women Uncle Sam had down as the sidesaddle assassin, with some justice, had been taking advantage of the local folk tale about a Twilight Lady. Longarm had once had a time catching up with land-grabbing white men pretending an Indian spook called the Wendigo was murdering reservation folks in their way. That black-clad figure on that big black show hunter had to be somebody taking advantage of a simple ghost story. Nobody real could have ridden the Mormon Delta at twilight for ten years without getting in trouble with the law much sooner.

Seeing he was headed that way, Longarm rode on over to the Lazy H to see how his other equine patient might be doing. On such dead-flat open range under a cloudless sunny sky, he was easy to make out at a distance. So a familiar figure came loping his way, sidesaddle, on a spunky palomino barb he'd never seen before.

As Polly Eastman whirled her new friend to fall in beside him, she gushed, "Aunt Olivia says she's mine to keep. I've named her Blondie, and isn't she precious?"

Longarm wasn't sure he wanted to hear the answer as he asked how poor old Dancer might be.

Polly said, "About the same, I guess. She dosen't seem to be getting better or worse. Jason still wants to shoot her, but Aunt Olivia says to give Dancer a chance, and Jason has to do what Aunt Olivia says if he wants to go on sleeping with her."

Longarm gravely said, "You hadn't ought to talk about your elders that way." And then, being human, he added, "You don't know who might be sleeping with whom, for a fact, do you?"

Polly shrugged and said, "I'm not allowed in Aunt Olivia's room after bedtime, but grown-up ladies like to sleep with men and Aunt Olivia doesn't have any other gentlemen callers, so there."

Longarm said, "I'd keep such guesswork to my ownself if I wanted my aunt Olivia to spoil me rotten. Why don't I have another look at your Morgan as long as I'm out this way?"

She said Dancer was alone on meadow grass lest other brutes fret her, or vice versa. She led Longarm east of the main complex to where he could see the sick Morgan, still sawhorsed near the wire of a fenced-in acre of grama and short bluestem starting to go brown.

Longarm reined in, dismounted, and tethered Sklark to a fence post before he ducked through the bobwire to assure Dancer he'd come in peace as he moved her way slowly but surely. She didn't seem to care.

He didn't have a thermometer handy. If he'd had one, there was no way he was about to shove one up a sick

113

pony's ass in front of such a young gal. He hunkered down to feel Dancer's inflamed hooves. They seemed no warmer, and as he felt her up, she lowered her muzzle to nibble some sun-cured grass. As he straightened up, he saw Olivia Hawker headed their way in a calico frock and sunbonnet. So he waited until the two gals were at conversational range to say, "She doesn't seem to be getting worse. That's the first step to getting better."

Polly turned to her aunt to crow, "You see? I told you Jason was just being mean and spiteful. I'm going to take Blondie over to the kitchen garth for a radish now, so there!"

As she remounted her palomino to lope off out of earshot, her bemused aunt asked Longarm if radishes would hurt a pony.

He said, "Not as much as sugar cubes, or even apples. You, ah, tend to ride her with a loose rein, don't you? Not that it's any of my beeswax."

The Widow Hawker sighed and said, "I suppose I do. She reminds me so of her mother, my kid sister, and Polly was so shattered when she lost both her parents at the same time."

Longarm grimaced and said, "Must have been rough on her. What was it, an accident?"

The orphaned child's aunt replied, "If only it was. Sudden death is bad enough, My sister and her man came down with the same yellow fever, and Polly was alone in the house with them when it started."

Longarm didn't ask for further details. The Mexicans called the same fever *vómito negro* because after it turned your skin yellow, you got to throw up black bile mixed with blood.

Nobody knew what caused yellow fever. But it always seemed to strike in warm damp weather along the Atlantic Coast or up the Big Muddy, as far as Kansas City, some summers. When he told her he'd never heard of yellow jack taking anybody in the Great Basin, she nodded soberly and said, "That's another reason I sent for her. Her father's family wanted to take her in. But they live in the District of Columbia."

That reminded Longarm who he was riding for out in the Great Basin. So he politely turned down her invitation for coffee and cake to remount and ride on back to town.

Once he got there, as he was rubbing Skylark down in Rachel's carriage house, Rachel came out back to ask what time she might be expecting him for supper.

He kissed her first and said, "Can't say. It's early yet. From here I aim to head for the county clerk's. Talked to a lawyer earlier who suggested some records I might go over. Unless I learn something astonishing, I'll likely get back here around supper time. No sense in pestering other folk whilst they're having supper, unless you mean to arrest 'em. But I'll tell you what. If I ain't home by the time you're ready to close for the day, you just go on and sup without me because it'll mean I'm tied up somewhere else."

Rachel purred dangerously, "Tell me who she is and I'll snatch her bald-headed!" She sounded as if she might mean it. So Longarm was glad his conscience was clear as he truthfully replied, "Ain't met up with anybody prettier than you here in Ogden. Ain't been invited to supper by even an *ugly* gal in Ogden." And this was the pure truth as soon as you studied on it. Neither Hazel Mullroony nor Olivia Hawker lived in Ogden and he hadn't planned on supping with either.

Dropping by the federal building, the sheriff's department, and the Western Union was a tedious time-consuming chore that had to be tended to. So business hours were winding down some by the time he made it to the courthouse to find the county clerk had left for the day.

But an auburn-haired gal in her late twenties, with those regular features just short of beautiful that made her look like kissing kin to half the folks in the Mormon Delta, said she was his recording secretary and asked how she might please Longarm.

He doubted she meant that the way it could be taken, although as she leaned across the counter at him, he could make out those square cutouts under her thin tight shantung bodice.

He told her who he was and what he'd come to paw through. She told him, "I can let you have last year's directory, sir, but some entries could be out of date, while this year's directory is about to come out at the end of the month."

Before he could ask a dumb question, Longarm remembered the first of July was the beginning of the fiscal year followed by most government agencies, and nodded, saying, "Last year's names won't help me. To be truthful, I ain't certain your new directory will right off. I won't know what I'm looking for until I go over it a time or two. Is there any way I can get myself an advance copy?"

She shook her head and said, "I'm afraid not, sir. As we speak it's being printed up. In Salt Lake City."

He said, "I ain't no sir. My friends call me Custis."

She smiled, and looked a tad less Mormon Delta, as she said that in that case he could call her Esther Harrow, and added that she'd heard that some called him Longarm.

He said, "Mostly newspaper reporters and crooks, Miss Esther. Might you be a newspaper reporter or a crook?"

She laughed—it made her prettier—and said, "Touché, ah, Custis. Would it do you any good to look at loose carbon copies of the pages I typed up for the print shop in Salt Lake City?"

He allowed it surely would. So she glanced at the wall clock, wrote something on a slip of notepaper, and handed it across the counter to tell him, "My place is just up the street and I'll be leaving here in a few minutes, if you'd care to drop by. I did the typing at home after hours and that's where I have the carbons, see?"

He said he did, and suggested, "Why don't I just wait here and walk you home then?"

She glanced away and blushed as she murmured, "That might not look right to some people here in town."

He didn't pursue the matter. Some Mexican gals didn't care to be seen on the street with a *chingado gringo* either.

But after he'd left and taken time to study on her offer without her smiling at him, Longarm recalled other Mexican gals who'd invited him home to meet their big brothers' gangs along the way. So, while it hardly seemed possible Esther Harrow was out to lead him into another Mountain Meadows Massacre, it was better to feel safe than sorry.

So Longarm found an observation position under the awning of a corner bookshop where he had a clear but discreet view of the side door she'd be coming out of, and sure enough, within a quarter hour Esther did come out, with a boater pinned atop her auburn curls and a big handbag under one elbow. She sure had a nice walk as she headed north without ever glancing his way. He gave her a lead, and stepped out to tail her from catty-corner on his side of the street. As he did so, a voice behind him snarled, "Hold on! I got a bone to pick with you, Denver boy!"

As the way more interesting Esther flounced ever farther up the far side of the street, Longarm turned wearily

to face Jason Kane, the ramrod of the Lazy H. You could
see the burly cuss had been drinking, and it hadn't done
a thing for his disposition. He snarled, "I told you Olivia
Hawker was taken, and you was out there again today!"

Longarm replied, "I was and what of it? There's nothing been said or done betwixt me and Miss Olivia that
I'd be afraid to tell her husband if he was still alive. But
for the record, if there *was* a thing going on betwixt us,
I fail to see what *you* might have to say about it. It's my
understanding you work for Miss Olivia as a paid employee. Are you trying to tell me you have any *other*
understanding between you?"

Kane scowled stubbornly and said, "She's my intended. She just don't know it yet. So you leave her the
hell alone or somebody around here is liable to get hurt
real bad, savvy?"

Longarm said, "I savvy you're an asshole beyond all
reasoning. So screw the reasoning and consider what you
just now did. You just now threatened a federal officer
on duty, packing a double-action six-gun and recalling
much less obnoxious pests I've been forced to shoot in
my time. So why don't you just turn around and walk
away, or if that don't suit your fancy, go for your fucking
gun and let's get this bullshit over with!"

Jason Kane stood frozen in place with his jaw hanging
slack. So Longarm said, "Make up your mind. I'm out
this way on serious business. I ain't done shit to you. I
ain't about to *take* shit from you. So get the fuck out of
my way or fill your fist. I mean it!"

Jason Kane must have decided Longarm did. He paled
and stammered in a fawning tone, "Aw, heck, can't you
take a joke?"

Then he turned to walk away, with his gun hand held
way out to the side, and that might have been that, had
not a high-powered rifle spanged in the distance to spin

Jason Kane on one boot heel like a clumsy ballet dancer to land flat and limp as a bear rug in the dusty street, whether dead or alive.

Longarm didn't pause to find out. He'd spotted the gun smoke above the rooftop across the way, and this time he knew better than to tear upstairs. Being on a corner to begin with, Longarm ran along in line with the building that rifle shot had hailed from. As he got to the building he met the gunsmith, Walt Beatty, on the walk near his own shop. Beatty yelled, "She went that way! Across the street and through that narrow gap betwixt the drugstore and that hat shop!"

Longarm tore past, yelling back, "Did you say *she*?"

The gunsmith called after him, "*Looked* like a she. Dressed in a black riding habit and packing that Keene .45-70 we were talking about!"

# Chapter 14

Longarm chased his questing six-gun's muzzle through the narrow gap, shiplap siding to the right and red brick to the left, to pop out the far end and crab to one side, braced for a bullet. But at first he saw nobody at all on up or down the narrower tree-shaded cross street.

Then he spotted two colored women half a dozen doors down, chatting half in or half out of the town house where one of them likely worked.

They broke off their conversation to regard him uneasily as he approached, six-gun in hand. He ticked his hat brim before he got to them, then announced he was the law and asked if they'd seen anybody else tear out that slot up the block just now.

They hadn't. They hadn't noticed *him* until he'd come tearing down the walk at them like that.

There was nothing to do but thank them, tell them he was sorry if he'd spooked them, and head back the way he'd just come.

On the far side of the slot, Walt Beatty had armed himself with a six-gun from his shop to meet Longarm in the middle of the street amid the gathering crowd. The gunsmith asked, "Did you get her?" And then laughed sheepishly to add, "I reckon we'd have heard. What do we do now?"

Longarm replied, "We scout yonder rooftops. The fire came from one not far from your own. Do you know the way up?"

Beatty said, "There's a stairwell to the roof in my building, next to my own entrance. We ought to be able to make it from one rooftop to another that way. She pegged a shot at you?"

Longarm said, "Ain't sure who she was aiming at. She nailed a ranch foreman named Kane."

As they legged it through the curious crowd, Walt Beatty gasped, "Jason Kane? Works for the Widow Hawker of the Lazy H? Jesus H. Christ, he's a customer of mine!"

Longarm headed for the narrow doorway next to Beatty's gun shop as he said, "We'd just finished talking, the next street over, when that crazy bitch let fly with her damned rifle. So I seem to have guessed wrong about her being too dainty for a .45-70, and ain't there an alley a few doors up too?"

Beatty said, "There is. But go on up and you'll see that where there's a will there's a way. Who on earth would want to shoot Jason Kane? He had his faults, but I doubt he had the brains to be in anybody's way!"

Longarm opened the door and led the way up the narrow stairs. He saw that, above the gun shop, narrow hallways in line with the stairs gave access to tenement flats of one size or another. A gray prune-faced crone leaned over the top-floor bannister to bitch, "What on earth are you children doing, running up and down these stairs like wild Indians, for land's sake!"

Longarm called up, "I'm the law and we're looking for the mischief-maker, ma'am. Are you sure you didn't hear her run *down* instead of *up* these stairs?"

The elderly woman complained, "Sounded like a buffalo herd running across the roof above me and down, down, down like a bowling ball on the stairs. It's not right to disturb a frail Christian widow woman like so as she's fixing to start cooking her supper! I'm so upset right now I may never feel like supper tonight!"

Longarm joined her on the landing, asking her gently to go back inside and lock her hall door. Walt Beatty said soothingly, "It's all right, Mrs. Austin. We just want to look around up yonder. We don't think she's likely to come back."

By this time Longarm had found the ladder leading to a trapdoor opening in the roof. As he holstered his .44-40 to climb out he saw right off what the gunsmith had meant about the alley between buildings. There was in fact a close-to-fifty-foot gap between most of the buildings facing opposite ways. Most, but not *all*. Beatty followed as Longarm led the way around the end of the blind alley to where he figured that rifle shot had come from. He knew he'd figured right when he caught spent brass gleaming in the late afternoon sunlight. He bent and picked up the empty cartridge, holding it out as he asked Beatty, "Same firing-pin pattern?"

As the expert on the subject took charge of the evidence, Longarm moved closer to the parapet and looked over it. He wasn't surprised to see a bigger crowd, including two county deputies he recognized, clustered around Jason Kane's spawled figure like flies around a fresh cow pat. He called down. When everyone looked up, he asked how bad Kane had been hit.

One of the local lawman called back, "As bad as it gets. We've sent for the morgue wagon. What are you doing up there, Longarm?"

The federal lawman called back, "Not much. She got

away. It was that same mystery woman in a sort of black Klan outfit. Only this time we're certain she was acting alone. Just now found her spent brass, and two witnesses agree she was up here on this roof alone!"

Since she didn't seem to be there now, Longarm suggested he and Beatty go on down and converse at easier range. Along the way, Walt Beatty observed, "Miss Olivia's going to take this hard. Jason's been riding for her since before her husband died!"

"You know her too?" asked Longarm.

The young gunsmith said, "Know her and just about everybody else in the market for guns and ammunition. Been serving her and her hands for years. Nobody off the Lazy H packs a rifle of any description chambered for Army .45-70 rounds, if that's what you're asking."

Longarm said, "Just like to touch every base as I run in circles. They're going to ask us both a lot of dumb questions at the coroner's hearing, Walt."

Beatty stammered, "Coroner's hearing? Whatever for? I don't know anything about poor Jason getting shot just now!"

Longarm said, "Sure you do. You saw the one who done it, and they're sure to want your expert opinion on that spent brass. So what's your opinion on that spent brass, Walt?"

The gunsmith said, "Looks like this one was fired from a bolt-action, and like I said, she was running off with a bolt-action Keene made by Remington, so what *else* might she have shot poor Jason with just now?"

Longarm said, "Hang on to the brass then. You can present it at the hearing when I show them mine. They'll probably summon us in the morning. Too late, right now, to round up a panel. First they have to wait for the autopsy results."

"They're going to cut him open?" Beatty grimaced.

Longarm said, "They have to." He opened the door at the bottom and added, as they stepped outside, "I know he was shot with a bolt-action rifle, and you know he was shot by a bolt-action rifle, but for all the coroner knows he was poisoned with flypaper soup."

Beatty asked how often autopsy results failed to match witness reports.

Longarm said, "Not often. Most times, when everyone says a man was run over by a train, he was really run over by a train. But every now and again they find a bullet in his messy remains, and have to call his wife and her lover back to go over it all again."

As they drew near, they saw Kane's cadaver being loaded in the morgue's black-paneled meat wagon. They joined the crowd, and one of the deputies told them, "Got both your names down for the sheriff and coroner. You say you have *two* witnesses, Deputy Long?"

Longarm hesitated, decided the attention might cheer her up, and asked Beatty to give them the details about the old lady on the top floor of his building. When he'd finished, the deputy, who'd been taking it all down in his notebook, asked where they might be able to find the both of them should anybody want to issue a summons.

It was an awkward question for Longarm. Walt Beatty lived over his shop, and said he'd be upstairs or down, most likely. Longarm wasn't about to admit he was sleeping with Rachel Hall. So he gave that hotel near the depot as his current address. He was still dropping by there for messages, so it wasn't an outright lie.

As the meat wagon drove off in the lengthening shadows, the crowd began to break up, and Longarm worked his way loose to leg it on back to Rachel's hardware. He found her alone for the moment, and told her what had happened just a few streets over. Rachel said, "Oh, my

Lord, what if you'd been the one she assassinated this time?"

He said, "We wouldn't be having this conversation. They're going to want to send me a written invite to the coroner's hearing. I told 'em I'd be at my hotel. So I fear we'll both have to sup and sleep alone this evening, honey."

She demurely replied, "I can close right now if you'd care to join me for an early . . . supper in the back."

He moaned sincerely, "That remark was cruelty to animals, and I'll keep it in mind and *git* you for it, soon as I can. But aside from protecting your rep, I have less delightful chores to tend right now. Still got some calls to make before bedtime, and there's just no saying what I'll find in my mail slot when I do get on over to my hotel."

Rachel asked, "Who might you be calling on this evening? Is she pretty?"

Longarm smiled thinly and replied, "I'd say she stood about six foot four or five, weighed about two-thirty before they started to drain her, and looks more like a he than a she."

She blanched and asked, "You mean you want to go look at that dead man, darling?"

He shrugged and said, "Don't want to. Got to. Such chores come with the job, but if it's any comfort to you, I'd rather look at *your* warmer body at any time of day or night."

It worked. He got out of there without ever having to lie to her about his invitation to Esther Harrow's place.

He went there first, seeing they'd likely cut Jason open after supper and take their own sweet time with the big stiff. The county clerk's recording secretary lived off down a cinder-paved and tree-lined lane in a one-story bungalow with a picket fence and well-kept garden wrapped around it.

Esther came to the door in a Turkish toweling bathrobe, with her curly auburn hair down. She looked flustered and said, "I wasn't expecting you this evening after what happened! I heard you were in a gunfight, right after we spoke at the office!"

He said, "Wasn't a gunfight, ma'am. More like a shoot-and-run-away-laughing. I can come back another time, seeing I've caught you in no shape for receiving this evening."

She said, "Oh, where are my manners? Do come in! I set those carbon copies aside for you the moment I got home. Then I heard about . . . gunplay and some man being killed and, well, I confess I set our supper aside and took a bath, hoping to get my appetite back before bedtime."

She led him through her compact well-kept bungalow to her cozy kitchen. She'd opened a back window to air the place, but you could still smell tobacco smoke. As if she'd read his mind, Esther smiled and said, "Handyman, putting up some shelves this afternoon whilst I was at the office. He knows he's not allowed to smoke in this house, but when the cat's away . . ."

"None of my beeswax, ma'am," Longarm said, suddenly aware of the three-for-a-nickel cheroots in his shirt pocket.

She waved him to a seat at her table near the window as she told him, "Yes, it is. I wouldn't want you spreading gossip about a woman alone with secret vices. You're a Gentile too, aren't you?"

He smile sheepishly and said, "I won't tell on him if he don't tell on me. I reckon you have to know what a craving feels like before you savvy how tempting it might be to smoke alone when the cat's away."

She asked how he felt about potato salad and cooled-off glazed ham with his buttermilk, seeing it was a warm evening and that might save some time. He said that sounded swell, and she commenced to deal out the light cold supper as she questioned him some more about that shooting over near the county clerk's.

It didn't take long to tell her all he had so far. He added that he meant to drop by the morgue later that night. He didn't go into details at the supper table. So he commented on her unusually swell potato salad.

She said, "Thank you. I have High Dutch neighbors and I like to try new things. I fear you Gentiles from other parts find our own old country cooking dull, with neither coffee nor dinner wine to pep things up."

He was too polite to reply that seemed the simple truth. The mostly Anglo-Saxon Latter-Day Saints had started out like the New Englanders with old English cuisine, if you wanted to call boiling everything to gray mush cuisine. Then, with all those strikes against them, the Saints had gone on to live with Paiute neighbors who found pinyon nuts and jackrabbit meat, with neither pepper nor salt, delicious. So most of the *country* folk of the Mormon Delta had been left out of the improvements in New England or Midwestern country cooking by all sorts of other folk with other notions of delicious. French cooks from Canada or fleeing events in France or Haiti had taught their new Yankee neighbors to at least spice up their boiled New England dinners with onions, herbs, and way more pepper. That swell apple pie American moms were now so famous for had been adopted crust and all from the Pennsylvania Dutch, who'd really come from Franconia in the heart of Herr Bismarck's Pan-Germanic Reich. Of late all sorts of German, Irish, Latin, and Jewish notions were starting to become "American" dishes, and of course, further south, pure Anglo cooks were commencing to have a contest with Mexico to see who could make the hottest tamales and chili con carne.

So Longarm allowed that his Mormon hostess made swell Dutch potato salad, and idly asked her how many such folks there might be out along their Delta now.

She said, "I'm not certain. A whole lot, I'm sure. They've dared to open a Bavarian beer garden here in Ogden, and our city council's fit to bust. I can show you those carbon copies of our new directory whenever you like. Can you tell just by the spelling of a name?"

He said, "A lot of the time. Not always. Some names, such as Hart or Singer, can be Dutch or English. Ervine and Myers can be Scotch, and leave us not forget the Irishmen named Cohen and Costello. But as a rule, when a family name sounds Dutch, it's likely Dutch."

So she served him some marble cake she'd never read about in the Book of Mormon, and then, dying for a smoke or at least some infernal after-supper coffee, Longarm settled down on a sofa in her parlor with what looked to be ten pounds or more of neatly typed, but sort of blurry, onionskin carbon copies of their new directory, loose and not in numerical or alphabetical order.

He soon discovered this hardly mattered. He just didn't know what in blue blazes he was looking for. Without disputed voters' registrations to compare them with, the sheets he was messing with only proved there were a lot of folks now residing in and about Ogden. He said he noticed they had nothing on the military post, *Camp* Ogden.

She sat down beside him on the sofa to pick up some loose sheets and sort of wave them around as she replied, "We don't have anything to do with the War Department, if we can help it. Camp Ogden has its own rolls of officers, enlisted men, and dependents, one imagines."

He said he imagined so himself, and confessed, "I fear

I've put you to some trouble for nothing, Miss Esther. Without an overall and total census, these scattered lists of names don't mean much, no offense. I'm sorry I wasted your time this evening."

Esther Harrow leaned closer, purring, "I guess I'll be the judge of how much time we're wasting, now that it's getting dark outside."

And damned if he couldn't see, as her robe fell open at that angle, that she was really wearing cotton flannel long underwear, scented sort of sultry with musky French perfume.

# Chapter 15

Longarm had long since found that women of every persuasion were as likely to want to or not want to in about the same proportion. But the different ways they'd been raised inspired all sorts of novel notions about slap and tickle. So while the first moves on that sofa started out as expected, Esther sprang some surprises on him once they commenced to grope one another sincerely.

She let him shuck her bathrobe, and it was true that that underwear was cut to expose a gal's crotch and nipples. But she wouldn't let him unbutten her down the front, and when he started to shuck his own duds, she wailed, "You can't mean to strip down *naked,* Custis!"

It was getting dark inside as well as out, with no lamps burning in her parlor, so he asked, "Why not? We can barely see one another in this light, and don't it feel friendlier in the buff?"

She protested, "What kind of a girl do you take me for? It's *wrong* to get naked, even when you're all by yourself! Didn't you know that, you . . . heathen?"

He kissed her some more, then kissed an exposed nipple as he ran his free hand down that fool flannel to her exposed crotch and told her, "I do now. Would it be all right if I stripped down to just my shirt, you modest little thing?"

She warned, "Be sure you leave your underdrawers on! You do have an opening to allow for sex down yonder, don't you?"

He dryly observed he hadn't bought underdrawers with a fly with sex in mind. But once he had his balls and all out of them, he rolled her on her back and, meeting no resistance, mounted her in his fool shirt and underwear, muttering, "Well, when in Rome . . ." He found to his delight that her sweet ring-dang-doo felt just as naked as any other gal's, once he had his old organ-grinder in her.

But the rest of him felt sort of left out as their cloth-covered bodies snuggled and slithered so sedately, and he had to laugh when she wrapped her long legs around his shirt waist, legs that were wrapped in cotton flannel.

She asked him what was so funny. He didn't think she wanted to hear those lewd jokes about wild Mormon orgies in long underwear. But once you got into such pleasures, it did feel surprisingly wicked. There was something naked as all get-out about turgid nipples thrust out at you through tiny square windows, and the contrast between her wet love-slicked groin and dry flannel-covered belly made it feel as if they were schoolkids having a piece on a porch swing with the grown-ups inside none the wiser.

Wherever she'd learned to be so shy about exposing her charms to even her own mirror, Esther had no qualms about getting on top or taking it dog-style, and it really looked wild to throw it dog-style to a gal in long underwear.

As they settled down on her rug for a second-wind cuddle, a shared smoke being out of the question, Longarm asked Esther how she'd ever taken that bath she'd bragged on, seeing she just hated to see herself naked.

She confided she bathed in the dark, there being neither windows nor a lamp to go with her indoor plumbing. Then she asked what he found so funny about that.

He kissed the part of her hair and assured her, "Nothing. Novelty is the spice of life, and Lord knows you ain't like lots of gals I know."

She giggled sort of dirty, and asked if he'd ever gone all the way stark naked with anybody else.

He said, "Only women. Naked men don't inspire me that way. I know this is going to shock you, Miss Esther, but you ain't the very first lady of your persuasion I've ever undressed, or tried to, and some other Saints seem more willing to get natural at times like these."

She sniffed and said, "There's nothing natural about being naked. It's uncivilized and sinful."

He asked her views on what they'd just done up on her sofa, and she demurely said, "*That* was natural. Weren't we able to satisfy our natural feelings for one another without stripping down like Digger Indians?"

He replied, "I reckon. I take it you feel that whether the Indians are a lost tribe of Israel or not, they're sincerely *lost*?"

She said, "The poor things have strayed further from the paths of righteousness than the rest of you dwellers in darkness. If you've really seen one of our girls naked as a savage, then she wasn't what I'd call one of our girls. Not a proper member of *my* congregation, if you know what I mean!"

He knew what she meant. He'd met up with Mexican gals who carried on more about going to confession in the cold gray dawn than the situation had seemed to warrant, and Pentacostal play-pretties who fussed at him for offering to squire them to a *dance* after he'd been in their britches could sound tedious too.

So after he'd tried in vain, in some interesting positions, to get such a conservative little Saint out of her holy underwear, Longarm told her that while he just hated to tear himself away before midnight, he had some wires to get off and a dead man to pay a call on.

They parted friendly enough, although she warned him not to get dirty when he tried to kiss her French-style. He suspected, as he left, that she might be just as glad to call it a night. Some kindly philosopher had remarked, French-style, that no man was ever more sane than he got after a good meal and a good piece of ass.

He suspected that likely applied to women too.

So as he strode off in the darkness of her unlit side street, he wondered idly whether she indeed felt as glad to call it an early night, and why that notion sort of pissed him off. It hardly seemed fair, but everybody wanted the final say in such matters.

He went first to the morgue, knowing the Western Union near the depot would be open all night. Inside, he found that thanks to his study of holy underwear, he'd missed the undressing and grand opening of the late Jason Kane. The all-night morgue attendant said everyone else had gone home and left the three stiffs in cold storage to him alone. That might have been why he was so willing to have company. As he led Longarm down to the cellar and along a dank corridor to where they kept the cadavers just above freezing, he explained the other two were a drunk who'd been run over by a dray and an old lady who'd died naturally but hadn't been found until she'd been stinking up her sewing room for a spell.

He used his candlestick to light the wall sconce in the cold gray room. The three bodies lay side by side under white muslin with their tagged toes sticking out. The old lady's toes were black. The attendant said lancing her bloated gut had helped a lot before the freezing ammonia-filled pipes running all around the walls had slowed her spoilage down. The lonely attendant whipped the cover off Jason Kane. He looked much the same as before, save for his poor color and the big Y-shaped incision sewed up with butcher's twine once they'd poked about inside him some.

The morgue attendant said, "I can tell you what they found. The cause of death was a .45 slug as tore through his aorta above the heart and lodged in his left kidney further down. The doc says he bled to death inside fast. The angle the bullet followed through him confirms the report he was pegged from a rooftop not too far away. Is that any help to you, Deputy Long?"

Longarm said, "Already knew where the shot hailed from. Wanted to be sure it went with that same .45-70 brass. Has anybody come forward to claim the body?"

The morgue attendant nodded and said, "His boss, the Widow Hawker of the Lazy H. We told her she can't have him until the county is done with him. She said she'd be back. She didn't seem pleased."

Longarm soberly said, "I heard she was fond of her foreman. I'll explain how coroner's inquests work next time I meet up with her. A lot of folks feel they have to do something, anything, as soon as they learn of an unexpected death."

They shook on that and parted friendly. Longarm went next to the Western Union to wire a progress report to Billy Vail and then some inquiries about Keene magazine rifles, chambered for .45-70. Walt Beatty had said he didn't stock any. Some arms jobbers he knew of farther east, and the Remington sales office itself, might know if anybody else out this way had mail-ordered the brand-new bolt-action in such an unusual caliber. Longarm had known before the gunsmith told him that Remington preferred to market rifles in their popular .44 caliber. Reaming out another hundredth of a inch to take the cheaper surplus Army rounds would be easy enough. But they'd only do so on special order. So it was worth some wires at night-letter rates.

When he got to his hotel he found that, sure enough, there were two envelopes in his slot behind the desk. One turned out to be a summons to appear before the coroner's jury come nine in the morning. The other was from Olivia Hawker from the Lazy H. She said she meant to attend the same hearing, she'd heard he was staying at the same hotel as she was, and asked him to come on up for a visit at any hour he got in, since she doubted she'd be able to sleep a wink all night.

Longarm doubted she'd meant after midnight, as it had gotten to be by then. But when he passed by her room number in the dimly lit hallway, he saw light under her door and, listening close, heard someone pacing back and forth in there. So he tapped on the door, and it popped open so she could gasp, "Oh, Custis, thank God you're here at last! I've been so worried about you! Where have you been all this time?"

He said, "Studying local customs," as he followed her inside. She shut the door and waved him to a seat on her still-made bedstead, saying, "They wouldn't even let me see poor Jason. Is it true he was shot with a high-powered rifle? Did it . . . mess him up a lot?"

Longarm took off his hat and sat down as he replied, "The bullet never touched his features, ma'am. You'll be able to treat him to an open-casket service, if you've a mind to, once they release the body to you. The coroner's crew were doubtless trying to spare your feelings until your undertaker can dress him proper. Nobody can touch a murder victim's body before the coroner's inquest has determined the exact cause of death."

She protested, "That's silly. Everybody agrees that

crazy woman who shot those census-takers shot Jason with the same rifle! Why does everybody have to be so *picky?*"

He told her, "They don't want to risk hasty findings when they have all the time they need to go over the details, Miss Olivia. What things look like and what things really are ain't always the same. I just now came from visiting old Jason at the morgue. He's reposing in cool dignity, his troubles are all over, and there's no need to worry about him until the hearing's over in the morning. The undertaker of your choice will almost surely be free to pretty him up and bury him most anywhere you say out this way, Miss Olivia."

She said, "My close friends call me Ollie. I'll be sending Jason home to his family in Tennessee. What did you mean about local customs just now?"

He made a mental note to mind his loose lip around a gal that sharp as he replied in a desperately casual tone, "Been looking into how many Saints and how many of us sinners might be voting out this way come November. I have it on some authority that whilst there are a few more Gentiles than Mormons here in Ogden Township, if not the county, the Mormons can be counted to vote in a block for their own slate, whilst the rest of you will be voting divided up betwixt at least three parties."

She said, "I don't get to vote at all and it's not fair. Would you take it the wrong way if I asked you to do something . . . silly for me, Custis?"

He allowed he'd try anything that didn't hurt. She sat down beside him on the springy bedstead and almost whispered, "I need someone to *hold* me. Just for a few moments with nothing more intimate in mind. I feel so scared and all alone tonight. I want someone to just hold me like my daddy used to hold me when there were monsters under the bed back home in Baltimore."

Longarm reached out to take the hurting widow woman in his arms. She buried her face in his shirtfront and whimpered, "Don't let it pull me under the bed and eat me, Daddy! Just hold me tight and make it go away!"

So he held her tight and kissed the part in her hair, murmuring, "Go away, monsters. I'm rough and I'm tough, I'm a whale of destruction, and I'm packing a gun!"

She laughed sheepishly and confessed, "I think you scared that one good! I'm sorry I'm being such a silly and . . . You sure smell awfully sweet tonight. Is that some fancy after-shave I smell?"

He said, "Hope so. Paid the barber two cents extra when I had him give me a shave and a haircut recently."

She decided, "You got your money's worth. It smells almost sweet as perfume. Please don't kiss the top of my head like that, Custis. You're a handsome devil and you know it, but I'm not ready to feel . . . that way just now."

He didn't answer. She sighed and said, "I'm sorry. I know you must think I'm teasing. Maybe I am. I feel so mixed up right now, but I don't think I want anybody to . . . go any further."

Longarm was sort of surprised at how easy it felt to assure her, "You'll know when you want to go further . . . Ollie. Don't you reckon you ought to try and catch some sleep now alone? We've both got a big day ahead of us come morning."

She sighed and raised her light brunette head to reply, "I suppose you're right. I'll be all right now, and thank you, Custis Long. I mean that from the heart."

He said, "Warn't nothing. You needed a little hug and I gave you a little hug. So nighty-night, sleep tight, and don't let the bedbugs bite."

As they rose together, she wrapped her arms around him, although in a sisterly way, to insist, "You know

137

what I mean. A lot of men might have . . . tried to take advantage when I fell apart like that. But I was hoping you were a gentleman of the old school with more will-power than most, and I see I was right!"

To which Longarm could only reply, "Yeah, must be something I had with my supper earlier."

# Chapter 16

Next morning, the inquest went fast because there was so little to talk about. A couple of others had heard the shot from above and seen Jason Kane spin and fall. So that let Longarm off. Walt Beatty was sure he'd seen that masked figure tear into the narrow slot with a bolt-action rifle, likely a Remington-Keene. Two deputies who'd gone over that same slot high and low testified they'd searched in vain for basement windows, hidden panels, and such. The deputy coroner, Melvin Klein, M.D., testified the bullet he'd dug out of Kane's left kidney was caliber .45, the same as the spent brass Longarm had found on that roof. Old Widow Austin, with a price tag dangling from her spanking-new summer hat, declared one person alone had run across her roof and down the stairs outside her flat, scaring her half to death. When it came Olivia Hawker's turn, she vowed Jason Kane had never said anything to her about being threatened by that Twilight Lady, and said she had no idea why the spooky figure had been scouting her Lazy H from a distance the other night. Nobody else came forward with any suggestions as to how Jason Kane tied in with those assassinated census-takers or a High Dutch hardware man the Twilight Lady had warned to leave town.

When it came Longarm's turn, he cheerfully confessed he didn't know why she might have wanted to kill Jason Kane, if she'd been aiming at Jason Kane, or how she'd vanished into thin air after doing so.

Longarm said, "I doubt it was anything tricky as secret panels. I suspicion that once we find out the answer, it will turn out to be childishly simple. This stage magician I used to know explained to me how most vanishing acts are so simple that the audience fools itself thinking up sneakier tricks. She told me about this one old boy who used to razzle-dazzle with his magic wand, waving silk kerchiefs above one big Chinese vase, whilst his assistant quietly stuffed things in another vase at the far end of the stage, in plain view but out of the spotlight. She laughed as she told me how slack-jawed the audience was when the magician pranced across the stage to start whipping stuff out of *that* empty vase as well. I suspect nobody saw a spooky black-robed figure pop out the far end of that slot because no spooky black-robed figure did."

The chairman of the panel asked, "Then you suspect she simply got out of that one outfit and sauntered off down the street in another?"

Longarm shrugged and replied, "I ain't made up my mind what I suspect yet. I got more suspicions than sensible motives on my plate at the moment. Have you ever trailed deer through tanglewood, sir?"

Half the older men on the coroner's panel had. So they followed Longarm's drift when he said, "It's tough when you spy a deer print here and another yonder as don't point nowheres, because you need more sign to connect the little you can make out. Assassinating them census-takers point one way. Running Klaus Pommer out of town points another, and I'll be switched with snakes if I can connect Jason Kane or the Lazy H with *either*!"

Another panel member asked him to go back over that *if* about the killer's choice of targets.

Longarm shrugged and said, "If I wasn't the target the other day, and if Jason Kane wasn't the target yesterday, somebody needs a whole lot of target practice. It's *possible* I was the intended target both times, and it's *possible* that sidesaddle assassin was scouting me and not anyone else off the Lazy H when she was spotted the other day and I was the one who chased her. But it works either way."

Walt Beatty, who'd had his turn but hadn't left, piped up with, "No it doesn't, Deputy Long. You're the law, out our way to look into that Twilight Lady's deadly doings. Poor old Jason was nowhere near you that first time she pegged a shot at you with that same .45-70. You *were* out at the Lazy H when she was spotted, scouting *you,* I'll vow, and you must have been the intended target yesterday because we all agree nobody in these parts had any sensible reason to gun poor old Jason! He was a ranch foreman. He wasn't trying to take a census or investigate anyone out to prevent the same!"

Longarm shrugged and said, "Neither was Klaus Pommer, far as I can see. We're missing something, Walt. Don't ask me what. If I knew, we wouldn't be missing it and I'd be making some arrests!"

The chairman must have thought they were arguing in circles. He banged his gavel and said he'd heard enough. Unless somebody had a damned good reason to argue, he was calling it murder in the first by a person or persons unknown and releasing the poor boy's body.

As the hearing was breaking up, Longarm found Olivia Hawker and Walt Beatty standing just outside the doorway. The gunsmith called him over to say, "Miss Ollie here says she means to ride back to her spread with that other lady still running wild!"

Aunt Olivia said, "I have to. I can't leave my niece alone in the house tonight. I rode in with two of my hands, and I'll be riding back with them, in the unlikely event that crazy woman on the big black horse would be interested in *me* to begin with!"

Beatty insisted, "You ought to stay here in town until we can be certain she's not. I know the kids you rode in with. I sold them the cheap thumb-busters they're armed with, and that killer in skirts took a rider ten times as tough! Talk to her, Deputy Long! Tell her to stay here in town for now!"

Longarm said, "I can't. It's a free country, even if she'd have to move to Wyoming to vote. As for the risk, in town or country, we were just attending the inquest on a killing here in Ogden. Corman and Lescot were drygulched out on the range. So I don't see as it's safer one place or another."

Olivia sounded like her niece, Polly, as she tossed her head and said, "So there!"

Leaving them to argue about it, Longarm consulted his notebook, and went afoot next to the headquarters of the local Democratic machine.

It didn't seem busy at that hour. The gal seated alone at a desk in the reception room looked anxious for company. She was petite and right pretty, with her piled-up hair as black as midnight and her eyes the blue of a sunny sky. She smiled up at him to demand in an elfin tone, *"Conas ta tu?"*

When Longarm just smiled down at her uncertainly, she sighed and said, "Sure and it was worth a try. For you're handsome enough to be Irish."

He laughed and flashed his badge and credentials at her. So she confessed to being Megeen Coyn from Connemora and said her boss, Himself, Boss Gallagher, was off on party matters in Salt Lake City.

Longarm told her what he'd come to talk to her boss about, and found himself musing aloud about her taking him for Irish, seeing his hair and mustache were almost as dark as her own.

She smiled and said, "Sure I don't have a mustache, you loon, and haven't you heard that where the hair is red the Norsemen tread? It's a dreadful mixture of strange blood you find in them big cities on the shores of the Irish Sea that were Norse trading posts before Brian Boru pushed them first unwelcome strangers out, and to meet the *true* Irish, it's along the west coast you want to be searching!"

Longarm politely but firmly pointed out that, as he'd already told her, he was interested in more recent history. He said, "I was hoping to get a line on the voting pattern to be expected out this way come November. I've been told the Mormons can be expected to vote as one for their own, whilst the slight Gentile majority in this one county may split their vote and lose as usual?"

She sighed and said, "Sure and I fear you heard right. We Democrats have most of the railroad workers, more than half of the cattlemen further out, and of course the Irish vote. The Republicans will have railroad management, most of the business community, and of course the Square Heads."

Longarm asked, "How come? I mean how come Irish immigrants seem to join your party whilst High Dutch-speaking immigrants drift as natural to the Republicans? I've already noticed they seem to."

Megeen Coyn sounded certain as she said, "Sure and you vote where you feel most welcome. We Irish had barely arrived as refugees from the Great Hunger when Lincoln's Grand Old Party was after drafting boys who barely spoke English into the Union Army. It was Democrats who led the resistance to the draft, and got many a family head a job with the city when there were still signs saying, 'No Irish Need Apply.' The Dutchmen, coming across the main ocean at about the same time to stay out of Prussian prisons, were mostly middle class or richer who brought lots of jobs *with* them. So they never suffered as much at the hands of the Republican majority, and as they learned to speak English, they began to *think* of themselves as members of the majority. Show me a real-estate man or merchant in Ogden who isn't a Dutchman and I'll show you a Jew. It's hard to tell their outlandish names apart."

Longarm said, "I'm pretty sure Klaus Pommer was Lutheran, but I'll check with someone who knew him, Miss Megeen. What can you tell me about your local Grange chapter?"

She wrinkled her pert nose and said, "*Aroo* and what about it indeed? The National Grange has no chapter out here on the Mormon Delta. For as dreamy as they are, they know better than to worry about a handful of registered Grangers in a sea of Latter-Day Saints! The National Grange is more an agricultural reform movement than a true political machine."

He frowned thoughtfully and asked if she'd ever heard of Lawyer Vogel just up the street.

Megeen Coyn smiled knowingly and said, "Sure and there be another dreamer of grand dreams. He has put together a small band of like-minded local Gentiles he calls a Grange Coalition. They say there's a bunch back East who claim to be a Mormon Temple too. I don't know how the National Grange feels about Lawyer Vogel. He seems to feel the only chance our three parties combined might have this fall calls for voting as one for the same non-Mormon slate."

144

Longarm mused aloud, "Don't see how the Saints can lose if everybody else splits their tickets."

She explained, "There's no argument about that. The sticking point is who the lot of us should be after voting for. We Democrats have our own boyos to promote, the Republicans would vote for Chinamen first, and Vogel's proposed realtors, merchants, and, naturally, lawyers none of us know anything about."

"In sum, it's a Mexican standoff and the Saints will win this fall as usual," said Longarm. It had been a statement rather than a question. But Megeen confided that Boss Gallagher had gone to Salt Lake City with some power-sharing deal in mind. She explained, "The Salt Lake Temple has bigger political plans than playing cock of the roost over this great dusty basin filled with mostly nothing at all and all. To get anywhere in national politics, the Saints are going to have to make some friends in high places who may not buy every word in that Book of Mormon. Have you ever looked through that curious tome, by the way?"

Longarm soberly replied, "I have. I like to read. There's parts of the Book of Mormon I'll just take with a grain of salt, like some of the tales in other Good Books. I asked this Fundamentalist preacher one time how murderous Cain went into the Land of Nod until he came to a city of men, seeing he was a member of the only family in the world at the time. The preacher told me I was bound for perdition and doomed to burn in hellfire forever because God loved me but couldn't abide such sassy questions."

He caught himself and reined in, saying, "I never came here to argue religion, Miss Megeen. But I thank you for clarifying the religious sentiments likely to effect the next election out this way."

He ticked his hat brim to her and went to Republican

headquarters, where he confirmed much Megeen had said, although this time with a fat old bird with mutton-chop whiskers and some really grand cigars for handing out to visitors.

At what passed for the local Grange chapter, he found Lawyer Vogel out, although the flirty Lilo seemed to want him to take her to lunch.

He passed on such a tempting invitation by pointing out he still had time for a few more calls before high noon. Lilo suggested she was always on tap for supper. You got the impression the poor thing was lonesome. He figured it was safe to assume Lawyer Vogel was screwing somebody else. He'd seemed too professional to mess with his hired help. Longarm had long since learned that men in positions of any authority could be divided into those too smart to give anyone on their payroll such an edge, and total assholes who thought with their peckers and wouldn't hire a file clerk they didn't get to slobber all over while working late at the office.

Longarm had lied to Lilo about other errands that late in a busy morning. He went back to the hardware to tell Rachel he was still alive and aimed to ride out to Camp Ogden that afternoon.

There were no customers in the front to be served at the moment. So Rachel turned her "Out to Lunch" sign to the glass, and locked up as she half sobbed, "I've been so worried and so . . . lonely. I confess I wasn't sure whether I'd rather some other woman shoot you in the back as greet you naked belly-to-belly out of my sight!"

He was able to assure her with a clear conscience that he hadn't rubbed his naked belly against any other naked belly, and added, "As a matter of fact, I did meet up with the Widow Hawker at my hotel last night. She was mighty upset about her dead lover, Jason Kane, and I tried to comfort her some. But feel free to ask her if we got to rubbing naked bellies or even kissing one another on the lips."

Rachel took his hand to lead him to his doom in the back as she said, "I might just take you up on that. I don't think Jason Kane was her lover, and her husband's been dead quite a while. Why do you want to go back out to that Army remount station, darling?"

He said, "Don't want to. Ought to. Got a livery pony out yonder that's costing the taxpayers two bits a day, and I could use my deposit back. If the other side hasn't figured out I'm riding a field hunter to match that big black show hunter, they just haven't been paying attention. So there's neither need nor profit in holding on to that smaller paint."

As she led him toward the stairs, Rachel asked in a small scared voice, "Does that mean you'll have no further need for . . . my carriage house?"

He assured her, "Got to stable Skylark *somewhere* till it's time to return *him* to his rightful owner. Can't think of a better place, or better company. Can you?"

Rachel said she surely couldn't, and hauled him on upstairs to prove it by broad day, stark naked, on top, and it sure beat all how naked one gal looked after you'd made love to another in long underwear.

# Chapter 17

Before he rode out to Camp Ogden, Longarm, walking sort of stiff, dropped by the county clerk's. Inside, Esther Harrow sounded sort of stiff as well when she said, "Custis, we have to talk. You know how I feel about you, but I've been thinking and, well, if you must know, a swain of my own faith if not your imposing build has been after me to see more of him."

Longarm resisted saying anything about long underwear, and just said he understood. He advised her, "Don't worry 'bout me. I'll just have to be a sport about it, Miss Esther. I hope you and the man offering you more of a future have a swell one. I mean that, whether you buy it or not."

Before she could change her mind, Lawyer Vogel came breezing in with a cigar in his mouth despite his surroundings, saying, "Thought I saw you turn in here, Longarm. My secretary, Lilo, tells me you wanted a word with me earlier?"

Longarm suggested they step outside. Once they had, he said, "You ain't supposed to smoke around ladies like Miss Esther. I ain't got time to go over all my natural questions about your plans for one big Gentile machine in this one county right now. I got to ride out to Camp Ogden to pick up a paint pony. On our way back I mean to swing south and canvas some of the settlers down that way about the so-called Twilight Lady."

Vogel asked, "How come? I understand both that census-taker and old Klaus Pommer were north of Ogden when she threatened them."

Longarm said, "She shot Corman's pard, Lescot, south of town, and after that, there's way more down that way. A spur railroad leading down to Salt Lake City. My survey map shows more smallholdings and fewer stock spreads down that way. A heap of farms further out run exactly a hundred and sixty acres, meaning they were claimed off the Interior Department under the Homestead Act, not granted as tithe holdings by the Salt Lake Temple back in the fifties."

Lawyer Vogel nodded and said, "You read maps good. Closer-packed homesteads mean more registered voters. I've been trying to convince them all, Democrat, Republican, or Grange, to forget party rivalries and vote as a Gentile block this fall."

Longarm said, "I heard. Boss Gallagher is counting on the Irish, labor, and smallholders' vote. I've yet to meet a banker likely to vote Grange instead of Republican. How many German-speakers might you have lined up to vote for your slate?"

The German-American politico said, "Not as many as I need, I fear. You're right about merchants and bankers of any ancestry. I've been trying to organize the country folk from my family's old country. But the literally stubborn Dutchmen keep telling me they don't mean to vote at all out here in Mormon country. They don't understand their Mormon neighbors, don't get along so well with the Irish or Paiute, and really dislike the railroad and banking interests. I've been trying to tell them, in *Hocht Deutsch*, how a vote not cast is a vote against oneself. But we're working on it and November's a long way off."

They shook on that, and Longarm walked back to saddle up and ride, feeling less stiff and way better about his love life, now that it seemed to be less complicated than he'd feared.

When he got back out to the remount station, he was allowed to belly up to the bar in the officers' club in his faded denim, invited to do so by a now-more-interested Lieutenant Colonel Walthers. Longarm filled the provost marshal in on what he'd learned so far, and while he was at it, asked how soldiers blue might go about voting in the coming nationwide and local elections.

The short colonel said, "On orders from the War Department, those of us stationed here in the Utah Territory won't take part in any local politics. Officers and enlisted men who may be U.S. citizens will of course vote for their own free choice of candidates for federal office here on the post. One ballot box for the officers and another for the enlisted men. What might this have to do with that crazy woman on a show hunter? And by the way, Captain Spooner has been asking about his Skylark."

Longarm said, "I'm returning the paint to its owner this afternoon. I ain't certain how much longer I may need the field hunter, and you can tell its owner for me that Skylark is one hell of a horse."

That settled, Longarm left Camp Ogden on Skylark, leading the paint, now rested to the point of frisky, on a long lead.

The afternoon breeze was off the Great Salt Lake to the west as Longarm and his pals headed for the post road at a northeast-to-southwest angle across open range.

In spite of the fact that he was still officially taking that census, Longarm now doubted any Mormons he canvased would be able to help him out about that mystery rider in black. The Twilight Lady *they* knew as a regional folk myth wasn't the killer of Corman, Lescot, and now Kane. If she was really a she, she had her own ax to grind, and had neither shot nor even threatened anybody who wasn't a Gentile from other parts.

So once they reached the southbound post road, Longarm rode right past the first produce, pig, and chicken spreads he came upon. He got out his survey map and consulted it as he headed on out to where newer homesteaders would have settled. It only seemed odd till you studied on it, but the slight Gentile majority around Ogden formed a Gentile hole in a Mormon doughnut, which in turn was surrounded by a bigger ring of far more recent arrivals. Longarm could see how tough it could be to build a disciplined party machine from townsmen you could keep an eye on and far-flung farm folk cut off from party headquarters by polite but distant Saints.

It took some serious riding before he turned in at the spread of a barley-growing man called Webber, Bert Webber, to get invited in for coffee and cake.

As Webber's mighty pretty wife or aging daughter served them, it would have been dumb to ask whether they were Gentiles. But Longarm managed to ask whether they were regular Anglo-Saxon Webbers or the High Dutch kind. Bert Webber said, "Bite your tongue. Do we look like infernal Square Heads? I'll have you know my family came from Essex Shire before the Revolution. What have we ever done to you to deserve such an awful suspicion?"

Longarm explained, "I was told a heap of High Dutch immigrants had settled down this way, and no offense, Webber can be either."

The man who bore the name, with some pride, explained, "Webber is an older Anglo-Saxon name than Weaver, albeit that's what it means."

Longarm allowed he'd just said that, and steered the conversation to whether Bert Webber was registered to vote in the coming elections.

The newcomer to the Mormon Delta shook his head and declared that it seemed like a whole lot of riding back and forth for so little promise. He said, "I don't mind the way the Republicans have been running things since we got rid of Grant's machine. Can't say I know enough about them Latter-Day Spooks to ever *vote* for any of 'em. So I'll just forget about next November and maybe vote in the next one, four years down the road, when we've got our bearings out this way."

Longarm asked Bert Webber what he knew about the plans of his near neighbors, native-born or immigrant. From the easygoing but ignorant answers he got, he could see Bert Webber just couldn't say.

So he thanked the lady of the house, whoever she was, and rode on, towing the barebacked paint like a pull-toy.

But he never made it to the next homestead, a quarter mile south. For off to the east, almost impossible to make out against the hazy foothills rising above the sage flats, that same lake breeze was stirring up a dust devil in the wake of that other rider mounted on a black show hunter!

Longarm let go of the lead, shouting, "Go home, Paint!" as he wheeled the bigger Skylark to lope east through the low chaparral. His move had not gone undetected. The distant sidesaddle assassin in black tried to get more distant, wheeling the show hunter due east, as if to head over the Wasatch Range at full gallop.

This time the so-called Twilight Lady had been caught in the open in broad daylight with no cover as far as Longarm could see. When he saw that other mount bounce like a rubber ball and keep going, Longarm was braced when, sure enough, he and Skylark came upon a north-south canal and sailed across it easy, even though it was over two fathoms wide.

"You can do it, Skylark!" Longarm shouted, whipping out his saddle gun instead of whipping an already willing pal. As if he understood, the big slate-gray hunter gave his all in a flat-out run on level ground, beelining through stirrup-high sticker brush as if it was no more than smoke.

But try as the gallant Skylark might, that lighter rider on that other gallant mount was slowly but surely increasing the distance between them as Longarm snapped, "Don't give it up, old hoss! I see she's moving like spit on a hot stove, but there's nowhere for her to run this side of the horizon, and we can always pray for a gopher hole!"

Longarm hadn't expected that prayer to be answered literally, and it wasn't. The other rider's Waterloo was a barb-wire drift fence, strung out across the middle of nowhere to keep range cows from drifting off to nowhere. Longarm would never know whether the fence had caught the other rider or her mount by surprise. To jump a four-foot fence, both horse and rider had to be prepared to go over at the same time.

They didn't. Not quite. That big show hunter flew over the drift fence as if he was going up and down on a merry-go-round pole. But as he came down on the far side, something went wrong.

As Longarm rode Skylark ever closer, the black show hunter they'd been chasing came down and kept going down, as if trying to follow a rabbit down a rabbit hole, before, seeing that wouldn't work, it somersaulted all the way over to land flat on its back atop its screaming rider, sidesaddle and all!

Longarm reined in short of the fence, and trusted Skylark to the grounded reins as he ran forward, Winchester in hand, to roll through the barb-wire as the other hunter staggered up on three feet, neighing, with its busted-up sidesaddle dangling. The black-robed rider the big brute had rolled over lay silent and still in a crumpled heap.

First things coming first, Longarm shot the poor brute, which had a nasty compound fracture of its near pastern. Then, as the busted-up mount flopped back down, Longarm cradled the smoking Winchester and knelt beside the rolled-on woman. He knew it had to be a woman. No man could have screamed that high.

He reached for her hood as he asked how she was. She didn't answer or offer any resistance as he slid the black poplin hood off. He could see she lay stone dead, staring up at him with a shy little smile. So he swore and declared, "Now, Lord, this just wasn't fair!"

But when he looked down again, it was still Esther Harrow from the county clerk's, with the color fading fast from her pretty face as Longarm said morosely, "Aw, shit, I thought you liked me. And all the time you just wanted to find out how much I knew. Or was the plan to murder me in my sleep and I fucked things up by leaving right after I fucked you?"

He wasn't surprised when she didn't answer. But it sure left him with a lot of unanswered questions.

He heard a distant hail, and turned to see Bert Webber headed out their way, bareback, aboard a dapple-gray plow horse. Longarm rose to his feet, and as the farmer rode within easier earshot, Longarm called out, "Sure could use the services of someone with a buckboard, Neighbor Webber."

Webber said, "You got that. Who's this you want me to carry into town for you, Deputy Long?"

Longarm said, "Her name was Esther Harrow. She rode herd on the record books for the county clerk, or she said she did. One of the first things I'll want to do after we get her to the county coroner will be to make sure she hasn't buried the county clerk under the stable in town she must have been keeping that big black gelding in."

Longarm said he'd explain along the way. As they rode together toward the post road, Longarm saw that paint had only run a few furlongs, dragging its long lead, to calm down and commence grazing off to the south. Longarm had told it to run the other way. So as Webber headed north toward his homestead for that buckboard, Longarm and Skylark rounded up the fool livery paint and headed after the helpful homesteader.

Once Webber had that same dapple-gray hitched to his buckboard, they rode back to where neither Esther nor her big black show hunter had moved an inch. They left the dead horse to be skinned out later, and loaded the busted-up Esther aboard the buckboard with her saddle and saddle gun, a plain single-shot Springfield .45-70 as it turned out, along with the Harrington & Richardson .32 she'd flashed at Vince Corman and Klaus Pommer, carried under her skirts in a garter holster over her holy underwear. The skirt under the black poplin outer layer was the same calico she'd worn to the office that morning.

By this time, other riders off other spreads were drifing out to see what all the fuss was about. So Longarm got to explain to half a dozen homesteaders as they all carried Esther Harrow into Ogden.

The trouble was, Longarm's explanations were as puzzling to him as they were to everyone else. Try as he might, he just couldn't make the pieces fit into any pattern at all, sensible or silly.

But going over it all out loud saved him some impossible guesses as he explained it all once more to the federal and local lawmen who gathered like flies around the county morgue as soon as word got around. As the morgue boys were peeling off her long underwear whether she wanted them to or not, a deputy who'd watched them load Jason Kane into that morgue wagon said to Longarm, "Didn't you tell us you'd just seen Miss Esther traipsing out of sight when a shot rang out from that nearby rooftop?"

Longarm said, "I did. She almost made it out of sight this afternoon before her mount bobbled a jump and crushed her."

The graying and bony Dr. Klein cut in to say, "That's not what killed her. She was shot in the back."

Longarm stared down thunderstruck at the nude cadaver lying on her side. He said, "That's crazy, Doc. I was there. I saw her horse come down awkward and roll with her!"

The deputy coroner shrugged and replied, "So who's arguing? You say she was rolled by a horse, I say she was rolled by a horse. But before she was rolled by a horse, somebody put a bullet right between her shoulder blades. See for yourself already!"

# Chapter 18

He did. Hardly anything but a bullet hole looked that much like a bullet hole. But as Klein probed the wound in Esther's smooth white back, Longarm insisted, "It just ain't possible! I was chasing her across open range in broad daylight. The chaparral all around was only stirrup deep. If I missed a distant rifle shot above the pounding hoofbeats, I still should have seen the gun smoke, and I never did!"

The deputy coroner held up a mangled blob of lead gripped by his forceps to opine, "Caliber .30 before it flattened against this unfortunate subject's spine. Probably a .30-30 varmint round."

Another county lawman suggested, "Try her this way. Say she never meant to swap shots in a running gunfight with a man of your rep. Say she was trying to lure you into a death trap, and had somebody staked out, flat in the sagebrush, betwixt that canal and that drift fence. Say the plan was for the pal to up and shoot you in the back as the two of you tore past. Then say that as the two of you tore past, in line, he missed you and hit her, just as she was fixing to jump that fence."

Another local rider chimed in. "Works for me! Getting hit and checking your reins just as you're supposed to be leaning forward and giving your horse his head sounds to *this* child like a swell way to boggle a jump!"

Longarm started to insist he should have heard the shot. But he didn't because it was obvious he *hadn't* made out the squib of a small-bore varmint rifle amid all that thunderous excitement off to the south.

He said, "Well, she sure was trying to get away, and she was only armed with a single-shot Springfield and that whore pistol against my way bigger six-gun and repeating Winchester. But she'd have been even better off not riding out after me at all! I reckon I'd like to check her bungalow, and above all the carriage house out back now."

Half a dozen local lawmen volunteered to help. He was glad to have them along. Seven pairs of eyes saw more than one, and it was one of the Saints who spotted the discarded cigar butts under the kitchen window.

Longarm sniffed one, observing, "She said she'd caught a Gentile handyman smoking when she wasn't supposed to be looking. It looks more to me as if some gentleman caller got to smoke all he wanted at her kitchen table. He'd have tossed the butts out the window at his side because she'd have naturally provided no ashtrays."

One of the Mormon lawmen frowned and muttered, "One of our girls with a Gentile calling on her?"

Longarm dryly suggested, "Anything's possible."

Another Saint snorted, "Good grief, the woman was riding about in that crazy costume, shooting people, and you can't believe she'd kiss a man who smokes?"

As everyone else there laughed, a volunteer Longarm had asked to scout around out back for signs of that big black show hunter came in to report, "Miss Esther was boarding her pony down the way and riding after work or on her days off. But they told me her pony's a bay Walker-Cob cross with four white stockings!"

Longarm said, "Makes sense. A woman alone with a job in town has no call to tend her sometime mount full-time. She was likely riding somewhere on her innocent bay in her innocent dress to change her duds and horseflesh somewhere else. Are they holding her bay at that livery, pard?"

The local lawman said, "Not hardly. They don't know where it is. They say she took it out for a canter this afternoon and never came back. I didn't think you wanted me telling them she was dead."

Longarm assured him he'd thought right, and rode over to that livery near the depot, leading the paint.

Once there, he asked the old Saint in bib overalls to put both his own nag and the borrowed field hunter away for him, explaining he had more riding to do on as fast a fresh mount as they could hire out to him.

The older livery man allowed he had a frisky roan cutting horse that could move some, but added it was no jumper to rival Skylark.

Longarm said, "I don't expect to be chasing anybody on a show hunter now. Just need stamina for some run-ning around in lots of circles this afternoon."

So they put his McClellan on a deep-chested roan mare with a white blaze who answered to the name of Blue Ribbon.

He rode first to the Democratic machine to tell the elfin Megeen what he needed. She said *their* copies of the directory were out of date, but he said out of date was better than just guessing, and left with a dog-eared copy they could spare.

He rode next to his nearby hotel to see if there were any messages there before he rode to the Western Union.

He found Olivia Hawker and Walt Beatty out front, waiting for her hired hands to bring her pony around from the hotel stable. She said Walt had persuaded her to get on home. The gunsmith's Tennessee show pony was tethered nearby. He'd changed to trail duds, and had an Army Schofield six-gun riding low and side-draw in a tie-down holster. He told Longarm, "We just heard you'd nailed that Twilight Lady. But I managed to convince Ollie here there could be more of them still out there!"

Longarm nodded soberly and said, "There has to be. One of them put a bullet in the Twilight Lady this afternoon." He ticked his hat brim to the young widow and said, "I reckon you will be safer out to the Lazy H, seeing you'll be riding home with a three-man escort."

She protested, "I'm curious as a cat, and I can't see why on earth that Mormon girl who works for the county clerk would have it in for me!"

Longarm said, "Neither do I. But you get along home and as soon as I tidy things up around here, I'll come by and tell you all about it before I leave the Delta."

Walt Beatty brightened and asked, "You're fixing to wrap the case up then?"

Longarm said, "I hope so. The pieces of the puzzle have commenced to fall into place. But you can't arrest nobody on what's likely. You have to present some proof. So I'm hoping for some at the telegraph office, and then I have a whole lot of fish to fry this side of sundown. So I'll be counting on you to carry this lady home whilst I ride a heap in other circles."

They didn't argue, although Olivia said she was holding him to his promise as he mounted the roan and wheeled away.

He didn't ride far. As he dismounted in front of the Western Union just down the way, he told Blue Ribbon, "I know you find this tedious, old gal. That's why I generally do such legwork on my own legs. But I'd look as dumb leading you all over town on foot."

He tethered his new mount to the hitching rail out front and went inside. The counter clerk said they did indeed have some wires on tap for him, sent from all over creation in care of Western Union.

He tore them open and scanned the yellow telegram forms for surprises. When he failed to find any, he consulted his pocket watch, saw it was going on four-thirty P.M., and headed back out front to get cracking.

Walt Beatty was dismounting near Blue Ribbon. He hailed Longarm and said, "I want in. I don't see why anybody would be after Ollie either, and she can make it home safe enough with her own hands. Who are we after? What did your other pals wire you?"

Longarm stuffed the yellow forms in a hip pocket and said, "To begin with, Remington Arms hasn't filled any mail orders for Keene magazine rifles rechambered .45-70."

The gunsmith and arms merchant said, "I told you she must have bought her repeating high-powered rifle somewhere else."

Longarm said, "When somebody shot her with a varmint rifle today, she was packing a single-shot Springfield Conversion. Didn't you say such a side-hammer rifle leaves a different pattern on the spent brass?"

Beatty nodded. "Of course. That's how I knew that brass you found on two different rooftops had been fired from a bolt-action with a dead-center firing pin. But hold on. If the Twilight Lady you just caught up with was packing a Springfield, couldn't that mean somebody else with a Keene was firing from the rooftops of Ogden Town?"

Longarm nodded soberly and said, "It couldn't have been Esther Harrow that last time. I'd just seen her vanish

way the hell up the street when Jason Kane caught that
.45 slug from a nearby rooftop. But then you said you'd
seen her tear-ass down them stairs and across the street,
to vanish like a rabbit down that slot across the way."

The gunsmith nodded but pointed out, "I never said I
saw a girl I knew from the county clerk's dashing all a-
flapping in that spooky black outfit. I said I saw *somebody* in that spooky black outfit!"

Longarm said, "So you did, and I've been wondering
about that, Walt. Why do you reckon anybody would
dress up like a haunt to run across daylit rooftops and
busy streets in the first place? Surely not to avoid attracting attention!"

Beatty shrugged and answered, "How would I know?
Do I look like a crazy lady given to assassinating all sorts
of gents with no sensible reason?"

Longarm said, "Oh, I'm sure you had your reasons for
wanting Jason Kane out of your way, Walt. Let me show
you something."

As he reached with his gun hand for the telegrams in
his hip pocket, he added with a sardonic smile, "How did
you fake that brass you left on the roof for me? Center-
punch in a padded vise?"

Walt Beatty went for his gun, seeing he'd never have
a better chance against a man of Longarm's rep.

Longarm had figured he might. So before Beatty's
Schofield .45-28 cleared leather, the double derringer
palmed in Longarm's big left fist spat considerable
smoke and just enough lead to drop the lightly built but
murderous gunsmith a good ways out in the street on his
back, with his own gun in the dust between them.

Longarm put away his smoking empty derringer, and
drew his .44-40 as he strode over and hunkered down to
determine what he'd just done.

The younger man he'd shot twice in the chest, point

blank, was still breathing, though barely. Beatty smiled weakly up at Longarm and said, "I was never after you. I *liked* you. What I did was done for pure love and the heart of a lovely girl!"

As others came their way from all around, Longarm soberly told the dying man, "I'll tell her, Walt. Jason Kane bulged his muscles at me, and I was never out to take Miss Ollie away from him."

Beatty coughed up some bloody foam and protested, "She was never his to be taken from him. He was just keeping all the other men in the Utah Territory from approaching with flowers, books, or candy. I had to set her free from the arrogant bully, and I meant no harm to another soul! What was it you were fixing to show me just now?"

Longarm said, "Nothing. I was hoping you'd slap leather. I had no proof and, no offense, I knew you scared easier than me. I'd just faced Jason Kane down when you shot him with that .45 *pistol* round, ran downstairs, and decided you'd seen the Twilight Lady run over into that slot. Had Jason been drilled at that range by a swamping .45-70 round, Doc Klein never would have found the slug still *inside* him. Had anyone at all run through that slot, those maids on the far side would have seen 'em coming out the other side. There was no other way in or out. My boss calls what I just pulled on you the process of eliminating. When you peel away all the other possible answers, you go with the answers you have left. But like I said, I needed proof."

Walt Beatty didn't answer. He was still smiling up at Longarm. But there was nobody home down yonder.

As Longarm was joined by other lawmen, drawn to the sounds of gunplay, one dryly remarked, "You sure are a noisy child, Longarm. Ain't that the gunsmith Walt Beatty you just shot?"

Longarm rose to his feet, pistol muzzle held politely, as he nodded and replied, "I had to. He was fixing to shoot me. Before that he shot Jason Kane, over near his shop. He must have seen Kane go by and saw a chance he'd been waiting for."

A county deputy gasped, "Well, I never, and who'd have thought it of such a prissy young gent! Was he the same one as pegged a shot at you and our sheriff from that other rooftop earlier?"

Longarm said, "I doubt it. I suspect that after I showed him some spent brass from that episode, he manufactured fake evidence to cover his premeditated murder of a romantic rival. I'm still working on who shot those census-takers, tried to shoot me, and then shot Esther Harrow with a lighter and less noisy varmint rifle."

The other lawmen exchanged uneasy glances, and one of them asked the federal rider, "Do you mean to say there's more to come?"

Longarm holstered his six-gun as he quietly replied, "I sure hope so. Two guilty parties, not all that wondrously clever but working at cross-purpose, had me mighty confused for a time. But with Miss Esther and now this poor lovesick loon eliminated, I've narrowed the field down to more chewable chunks."

One of the lawmen said, "Hot damn! Who are we going after next?"

Longarm said, "I ain't ready to say. I still need proof and, no offense, I've my reasons for respectfully declining local assistance. So why don't you all help me tidy up this shooting so's I can be on my way before sundown?"

# Chapter 19

Blue Ribbon was a not-bad cow pony with a steady mile-eating lope. But by sundown Longarm was riding a jaded mount with a saddle-sore ass. So as he rode her into the dooryard of the Vogelhorst, he told her he was sorry and assured her they were about done with loping for the day.

Vogelhorst meant Bird's Nest in High Dutch. The sardonic Lawyer Vogel's five acres on the outskirts of town were sort of grand for a suburban residence, and too small to call a spread. As Longarm dismounted out front, Lawyer Vogel in the flesh stepped out on his veranda to howdy him, saying, "Heard you caught the Twilight Lady and shot it out with her confederate, Walt Beatty. Might you be in the market for a good lawyer? The way I heard it, you couldn't be in any trouble over either death."

Longarm tethered Blue Ribbon and strode over to join the property owner by his doorstep, saying, "That love-sick gunsmith wasn't in with Miss Esther Harrow. They barely knew one another. They were dealing different games at separate tables, and I don't mind telling you they had me as mixed up as a Denver omelet."

Vogel asked, "Then what can *I* do for you? Come on

inside and we'll talk about it over brandy and cigars."

Longarm said, "I'd as soon pass on both just now, no offense. Still have a long night ahead of me, and I'm so stiff from riding I'd as soon stay on my feet for a spell. Did you know that when you spell Corman with a K it's a High Dutch name, like your own?"

Lawyer Vogel nodded easily and said, "Now that you mention it, I suppose Vince Corman could have been German-American, if you want to suspect him of . . . what? I never spoke to Vince Corman in any tongue before Miss Esther or that sneaky gunsmith shot him . . . for doing what?"

"Speaking High Dutch," Longarm replied. "I just verified that with a wire from his kin back East. He'd changed the spelling to fit in better. But he was a second-generation Korman who'd been brung up speaking fluent High Dutch, just like Klaus Pommer was able to as he drove his peddler's wagon all over the Delta's back roads."

Vogel said, "Nobody shot Klaus Pommer. I understand he's alive and well out Frisco way."

Longarm nodded and said, "I checked up on him too. Ain't the modern wonders of Western Union grand? Nobody *had* to shoot Pommer when he heeded that warning to leave these parts forever. Vince Corman was dry-gulched because he ignored the warning. His sidekick, Lescot, was shot at the same time or sooner to make the motive less obvious."

Longarm became aware of shadowy figures standing at both ends of the veranda now. They'd doubtless circled the house from the back door. Meanwhile, Lawyer Vogel quietly asked, "What motive are we talking about, Deputy?"

Longarm said, "I just told you. Vince Corman spoke High Dutch. I don't. But I've already found out few if any recent immigrants from any old country mean to vote or even register to vote in the coming fall elections. November can be colder than a witch's tit out here in the Great Basin, and this Army man I know says they'll be setting up two separate balloting places at Camp Ogden alone. So ain't it safe to assume that, come November, there'll be at least a dozen ballot boxes to stuff, spread hither and yon across a thirty-by-thirty-mile county?"

Vogel didn't seem to be making any signals Longarm could spot. But now there were *four* others looming silently in the gathering dusk as their host, or boss, told Longarm, "There could be more. But all the polling places will be guarded by joint poll-watching committees made up of all the political parties on the ballot."

Longarm said, "Well, sure they'll be watching all them ballot boxes. But watching for whom? Strange faces they've never seen before? Sure, most of the folks right here in town would be tough to fool with ringers, but out across the Delta, where Saints don't sip tea with Gentiles and nobody knows what them fool Square Heads are saying . . ."

"What you're suggesting just won't wash," the German-American politico insisted. "This isn't a big-city slum or a backwoods hollow in the Ozarks where one party alone oversees the so-called elections. We're talking about real political *rivalry* out *our* way, and you can't get away with paying drunks to vote early and vote often. Nobody will be handed a ballot to mark and drop in the slot, with everyone looking, unless he's been registered to vote at that very polling place!"

Longarm nodded agreeably and said, "That's why you didn't want Vince Corman nor Klaus Pommer explaining American election procedures in High Dutch to ignorant immigrants. Your plan wouldn't have worked worth shit had even a dozen greenhorns come in to register themselves after you and your bunch had *already* registered them."

There came a long silence. Then Lawyer Vogel decided, "It's just as well you refused to come inside. I just put down a new Brussels carpet. Are you aware of the ramifications of that accusastion, you clever child?"

Longarm said, "Sure I am. If stuffing ballot boxes was a capital offense, half our government would have been hung by now. But to get away with electing a minority slate with even a narrow majority of the official rural vote, you'd have to cram them boxes with more ballots than there'd be if you could register every immigrant name out this way fair and square. So you had to make up *extra* names out of whole cloth, getting Esther at the county clerk's to help out by filing them as county residents. You knew long before I did that her boss is away from the office a heap, treating his delicate nerves with ninety-proof patent medicine."

One of the others took a step closer. Lawyer Vogel shook his head and said, "I want to hear him out first."

He turned back to Longarm to ask, "What else have you guessed about that Mormon girl and me, seeing you seem so anxious to get it all off your chest?"

Longarm said, "Shit, who's guessing? Thanks to your expensive taste in cigars, I knew right off someone had been smoking the same brand in her company. We both know you ordered her to razzle-dazzle me with meaningless carbon copies and fuck me to find out how much I knew. She sure took orders good, but I sort of wish you'd told her to take off that long undewear."

Lawyer Vogel laughed despite himself, recovered, and purred, "You do like to play with fire, don't you? But keep talking. What else do you know about that country girl and me?"

Longarm said, "I noticed she seemed a little country.

168

You filled her head with visions of sugarplums and got her to play at riding all in black, on that show hunter you must have been keeping out here. So where's the Walker-Cob with white stockings she rode out here earlier this very day?"

Vogel said, "In the stable out back with the rest of the stock. I asked what you knew about *her* not her damned *horse*!"

Longarm asked, "Shit, don't you know? You were the one who told her to warn off them census-takers, lest their census figures conflict with the county records she'd been cooking for you. Was it you in the flesh, or one of these other morose individuals I can't help noticing, who shot Vince Corman and then aimed that shot at me in CourtHouse Square lest I get too warm?"

Lawyer Vogel sighed and said, "I feared you'd get too warm as soon as I heard you'd be on the case. I sent one of my boys to head you off in Denver, and you somehow pulled the wool over his eyes. I was afraid you might. What makes you so sneaky, Longarm?"

The lawman, who was covered from more than one direction now, laughed and said, "Coming from you, I'll take that as sheer flattery. But how could you have known I'd be assigned to the case, and sent your gun by rail at the same time Supervisor Wortham must have still been aboard his own train from the East?"

Lawyer Vogel stuck out his chest a tad and smugly replied, "A man in play-for-keeps politics has to keep his ear to the ground. If it's any comfort to you, the National Grange troubleshooter who wired that we could be in trouble didn't know what was going on out our way. He simply advised that they'd be sending someone good and that it was time to wash any dirty linen we didn't want to explain. There's ever and always spots to tidy up when company is on the way."

Longarm said, "I know. I used to have to get ready for a fool Army inspection in a hurry. But how did you know it was me they'd send out here?"

Vogel said, "You have a Mormon admiration society. When I heard they'd be sending the best, I asked my friend the sheriff who the best might be. He said you knew Sarah Bernhardt too. But frankly, now that I've seen you in action, I don't see what all the fuss was all about."

Longarm modestly replied, "Miss Bernhardt never made no fuss when I asked if the sheriff and his womenfolk could have passes to see her show. I was tagging along as her bodyguard at the request of State, and she'd come to rely on me for advice in getting along out this way."

"*Gott im Himmel* and fuck Sarah Bernhardt!" Lawyer Vogel declared. "I meant I failed to see why they thought you were so good. I watched you flounder around like a rooster with its head cut off!"

Longarm said, "I had help. With you willing to have your girl screw me to cover your tracks after you'd almost got her caught, too early in the evening, and not knowing I had a field hunter that could jump canals as good as your own. You sent her out *that* time to convince me there *was* such a rider and it was not just a made-up Mormon fairy tale. Then, however, she was blamed for the killing of Jason Kane. You thought it was time to break off your . . . ah, relationship."

"Now how might I have done that?" purred Lawyer Vogel.

Longarm asked, "Don't you know? You gave the orders. Poor dumb Esther didn't know the whole plan, of course. She'd have never tried to lure me out past one of your boys staked out with that .30-30 had she known he had orders to kill *her* and let me jump to a whole heap of false conclusions. But she didn't, and to tell the truth, I'm a mite pissed. I thought she liked me more than that, even though I never got her to take off her underwear. Was that another reason you had her killed, Lawyer Vogel?"

The politico seemed to coil like a snake as he snarled, "I had her killed because she was stupid enough to fuck you. I never *told* her to fuck you. And I've heard enough. Why don't we all stroll around to the barnyard now? I have a garbage pit I'd like to show you."

Longarm absently reached for a milder smoke of his own as he calmly replied, "I reckon I've heard enough too. Franz Vogel, Esquire, I am placing you under arrest for the murders of two federal census-takers and a gal who might have made a swell witness once we'd offered her some immunity!"

Vogel snorted in disbelief and snapped, "Like hell you are! Kill him, Karl! Kill him here and now!"

Nothing happened. The blurry figures at either end of the veranda just stood there as the boss crook shouted, "*Was ist los?* So why are you all just standing there? Didn't you hear me say to kill him?"

Longarm said, "They heard you. But they ain't taking orders from *you*, Lawyer Vogel. I brought 'em over from Camp Ogden to back *my* play."

As the thunderstruck mastermind realized those were brass buttons down the fronts of the dark figures he'd taken for his own men, he shouted like a barefoot boy who'd stepped on a nail, and made a mad dash out across the dooryard as Longarm yelled, "Don't do it! Hold your fire!"

Then a single pistol shot rang out, and the running man staggered on a few paces before landing on his gut to flop around on the dusty ground like a circus seal, for a strangled scream or two.

Lawyer Vogel lay flat on his face by the time Longarm got to him, knelt, and rolled him over to feel his throat and mutter, "Aw, you're no fun. But thanks to my M.P. pals getting the drop on *your* pals as they came pussy-footing out the back, more than one of them figures to turn state's evidence against you and the one or more of their pals who'll get to hang for certain."

Lieutenant Colonel Walthers strode out across the dooryard to join them, his own smoking Schofield in hand as he gleefully asked, "Did I kill the murderous son of a bitch?"

Longarm quietly replied, "You sure did. And I was just commencing to think you might not be a total asshole after all! Didn't we both agree it would be best to take them all alive if possible?"

Walthers sniffed and said, "I agreed to help for mention by name in your official report, and he was about to get *away,* damn it."

"Away to where?" Longarm asked as he rose to his feet, dusting off one knee as he sighed. "Never mind. What's done is done, and I'll want you and your men to agree in writing to his guilty knowledge and an open death threat at the last."

The short colonel yelled for his sergeant of the guard, and once the three-striper ran out across the dust to throw him a snappy salute, the imperious officer pointed at the body with the muzzle of his six-gun and said, "I want this cadaver wrapped in a tarp and delivered to the ci-vilian morgue in Ogden. This civilian peace officer is going to prepare some statements for you and the other men of this guard detail to sign. Instruct your men to just sign them, with no further discussion. Are there any ques-tions?"

The noncom said, "Yessir. About the prisoners. Do we

take them out to our own stockade or turn them over to the civilian authorities?"

Without consulting Longarm, the Army man snapped, "We march them out to our camp and hold them there under guard until such time as we get further orders from Washington. Carry on."

As the sergeant of the guard trotted off to carry out those orders, Longarm quietly said, "All right, you ain't a total asshole after all, Colonel. I was afraid I might get stuck out here for the duration of their trial."

Lieutenant Colonel Walthers nodded grimly and said, "So was I, and I feel better with that Continental Divide between us, if you don't mind my saying so."

Longarm didn't mind his saying so. It was a thundering wonder how two men who couldn't stand one another could be in such total agreement.

# Chapter 20

They found seven rifles on the premises. Three Winchesters, a Bullard lever-action repeater, a Springfield Conversion like the one Esther Harrow had been carrying, the Remington .30-30 varmint rifle that had killed her, and one Remington-Keene special with eight rounds of .45-70 in its tubular magazine.

Esther's horse was out back with eight others. Three of Vogel's followers who'd been disarmed in the backyard as they came out the kitchen door said they were innocent immigrant lads led astray by a slick-talking Yankee lawyer, and agreed the fourth rider, Karl Schumacher, who kept swearing they were full of shit, was the gunman who'd been shooting at everybody on Lawyer Vogel's orders.

Later, it being an election year, there was a little fussing and fuming over jurisdiction, but everyone finally agreed to let the county have the glory of six inquests, with the coroner finding that since Corman and Lescot had been federal employees, and since there was nobody alive to try for the murders of Jason Kane or Esther Harrow, and since Walt Beatty and Frank Vogel had been killed lawfully by federal lawmen, it made good sense and saved the county money to let Uncle Sam try Karl Schumacher for whatever in tarnation he'd done, and refrain from confusing the voters further.

So Longarm was free to leave the Delta, and parting could be such sweet sorrow dog-style with as good a sport about it as old Rachel Hall. She didn't ask, so he had no call to tell her he wasn't going directly to the railroad depot as she opened for business that last morning they had together. She was able to open a tad late because her sale had gotten her out of the red and business was slacking off to slow-but-steady.

That military police detail had taken Skylark back to Camp Ogden along with their federal prisoners. Longarm had returned Blue Ribbon to the livery before walking home to Rachel after midnight. So he got to tote his saddle and possibles back the hard way, and left them in the tack room at the livery after he'd reserved one of those retired Army bays for later.

The dozens of minor errands he had to tend to in order to leave the Mormon Delta with nobody sore at him used up the rest of the morning, and got him to walking less funny by dinnertime.

He treated himself to steak smothered in onions with strong black coffee at a swell sit-down restaurant run by and for Gentiles across from the depot. It felt more luxurious than lonely. A man who led a tumbleweed life was forever surprising himself that way. Sometimes it felt just awful to find oneself alone in a strange town, but on other occasions there was almost a guilty pleasure in not having to ask anyone, male or female, how they felt about that serviceberry pie on the dessert menu or another cup of coffee.

After a run of luck with the ladies, a man could get a swell hard-on sliding between clean hotel sheets alone, knowing he was free to go right to sleep and never have to fight for the covers or explain why he had to get up in the dark to pee. The shifting moods inspired by such living could inspire a man to think twice before committing himself to the vows of a monk or matrimony. Longarm had it on good authority that many a happily married man suffered moments when he wished he was single, and Longarm already knew what it felt like to suffer celibacy, or a clinging vine who'd looked a lot better when you asked her for that first dance.

So once he'd checked one last time with Western Union, settled up with the hotel, and saddled up that antique Army bay called Kiowa, Longarm felt no call to stop by Hazel Mullroony's shop along the way. She'd asked him not to anyhow, and thanks to the way good old Rachel had served his breakfast, he just couldn't see why men or women went to so much effort for such fleeting pleasure.

But the Lazy H was out a ways, and after a few hours rocking back and forth in a split-seat McClellan had restored some circulation, he was just as glad he'd promised he'd call on the handsome Widow Hawker before he left aboard that night train to Cheyenne.

Young Polly Eastman spotted him from afar, and loped her palomino out to greet him. As she fell in beside him, Polly said, "Aunt Olivia says you shot that wicked Walter after he'd shot Jason, and now who's going to be Aunt Olivia's boyfriend?"

Longarm said, "There you go again. Neither one of them was her boyfriend, sis. Poor Walt just wanted to be, and Jason wouldn't let him court her. How's Dancer coming along with that laminitis?"

Polly said, "I think Dancer's a little better. This morning, when I visited, Dancer came over to the fence, nickering for a sweet."

"Good grief, didn't you remember what I said about that?" Longarm sighed.

Polly said, "Of course I did. I told Dancer to behave and just eat sun-cured meadow grass for now. Do you want to be Aunt Olivia's boyfriend?"

Longarm quietly explained, "She made me promise to drop by and bring her up to date on the troubles in town before I left. I'll be leaving well before sundown to catch a train, and you ought to learn to control your tongue if you can't control your imagination!"

Polly replied, "I'm not imagining anything. I know what grown-ups want to do to one another when nobody's looking. Aunt Olivia told me not to watch when our studs serviced our mares, but I peeked and it made me feel sort of . . . funny."

Longarm bit his tongue. It wasn't for a grown man who wasn't her kin to warn her about talking like that to grown men who weren't her kin—or for that matter, who were kindly old uncles.

As they neared the house, Aunt Olivia came out across the dooryard in her own riding habit, calling out, "Thank heavens you're here at last. We've heard so many conflicting stories about last night, and is it true you had to shoot Lawyer Vogel?"

Longarm reined in to lead the bay afoot, beside her, as he modestly said, "I wanted to take him alive. He was shot by a hair-trigger Army officer who's never had a lick of sense."

She said, "Well, come on inside and have some supper wine I've been saving for some big occasion. You're the biggest occasion we've had out this way for some time and . . . Polly, dear, don't you want to ride Blondie some more?"

Polly said, "She's had enough exercise for now, and I want to hear all about that gunfight too, so there."

Her aunt told her, sweetly but firmly, "She needs to be watered, rubbed down, and curried then, if you mean to keep two ponies of your own on this spread, young lady. In the meantime, Uncle Custis and I may ride out a ways for a private conversation. You remember what a private conversation is, don't you, Polly?"

The pretty little sass said, "I know how horses and other critters carry on in private too, so there!"

Ollie blushed a becoming shade of rose and snapped, "Another word and you'll be locked in your room with no supper, young lady!"

So Polly allowed she'd been meaning to curry her palomino, and as she rode off, her embarrassed aunt told Longarm, "I'm afraid she's at an awkward stage. Why don't I put that wine in a picnic basket and let me show you a secret treasure hidden by the silvery sage?"

Longarm repeated what he'd just told Polly about that train. But she promised to send him on his way before sundown. So he and Kiowa just waited outside a few minutes while she fixed up that picnic basket.

Then he walked her toward the stable, leading his own mount. One of her hired hands came out, leading a cordovan gelding sidesaddled. Longarm had already suspected he'd been expected out this way.

They both mounted up and rode off toward the purple mountains smiling over the eastern horizon.

Along the way, since she kept asking, Longarm told her, "In the beginning there was an ambitious political outsider who saw a chance to steal an election with the community divided into factions that hardly spoke to one another. He'd seduced and recruited a frustrated and underpaid recording clerk at the county clerk's office. Betwixt them it was simple to doctor the county records to where they'd agree with him when he registered a whole bunch of immigrants who didn't exist at all or didn't know enough about our ways to be interested in registering their ownselves. The survivors of his plot confessed last night that they meant to recruit hobos and saddle tramps this fall to vote early and often, at more polling places than one, under false, mostly Dutch, names. How many regular Americans, Saint or Gentile, might challenge a strange face named Snicker Fritz or Tanning Bomb?"

"Not I!" confessed Ollie with a light laugh. Then she asked why Lawyer Vogel had gone crazy.

Longarm said, "He knew what he was doing, albeit it must have had him fit to be tied when first a High Dutch-speaking peddler and then a second-generation census-taker who spoke the same lingo proceeded to ride around telling immigrants they ought to register and vote."

Ollie pointed her riding crop to say, "Over that way. Is that why they tried to scare those unwelcome Dutchmen off with a local legend of the Delta?"

As he followed her lead Longarm said, "Misdirection. Vogel knew his obvious motives might stick out like a sore thumb if he just up and drygulched everybody. They were banking on Vince Corman to report the threat from a local haunt before they got around to gunning him. That's why they did so after they'd already taken out his partner, Lescot. They had more luck with Klaus Pommer. Knowing for certain that a sidesaddle assassin had backed up her threats against Corman and Lescot with bullets, he just ran for it, and they never had to murder him. Lawyer Vogel was desperate, not crazy-mean. They thought it best to kill me, more than once, because they'd heard I got along well with rival factions out this way and knew the way local politics worked. When they missed me first in Denver and then Ogden, they let me spot that mystery woman to prove she was real. They never expected me to chase her on another hunter that could jump as well as her own, so we had one another on edge, and they'd have doubtless tried for me some more if poor lovesick Walt Beatty hadn't led me astray from their sign by gunning your ramrod, Jason, and fibbing a lot to me. Once they saw I wasn't even warm, they proceeded to play me like a sucker fish. Figuring he had me all mixed up, Lawyer Vogel decided to *give* me his sidesaddle assassin, dead, figuring as long as she never told me, I'd never be able to connect her to him. But he was wrong, and the rest you know."

Ollie replied, "The devil you say! Forget about dirty politics. Whatever possessed poor Walter to murder poor Jason over me? I'd never given either a word of encouragement!"

Longarm said, "I already figured that. Jason acted way too possessive for a man who possesses all he wants. Walt Beatty wanted to court you, but he was scared skinny because Jason could be scary as all get-out and Walt barely came to his belt buckle. So when I brought evidence from a sincere assassination attempt to Walt for his professional opinion, he told me true I was looking for somebody with a bolt-action .45-70. Then, knowing we'd never tie *him* in with such a weapon, he faked a spent cartridge by drawing the slug and detonating the cap with a center punch at his workbench. He kept it handy and bided his time until he saw his chance. His chance came, and he scampered across the rooftops and down the stairs to tell me a big fib when I tore round the corner to confront him. He fooled me because, as he was banking on, I thought I was after somebody with a rifle."

Ollie said, "Here we are," as she led them out of the chaparral to the wide but shallow pool of cool water where two canals met like secret lovers, far from anywhere else.

As they dismounted to tether their brutes, Ollie asked

why Walt Beatty had slapped leather on Longarm after fooling him like that.

Longarm said, "*I* fibbed to *him* that time. I implied I was getting warmer than I was, and misdirected him with my gun hand. Once I had him and poor dumb Esther Harrow out of the picture, I commenced to put the pieces left on the table together. But I had to misdirect Lawyer Vogel some before I could prove my educated hunch."

Ollie said to remind her to never try and trick him as she spread a picnic blanket from her saddlebag on the clean sand by the pool and sank down on it to commence spreading cold cuts, two kinds of bread, and that bottle of dry red Burgundy for his approval.

Longarm approved a lot as he tossed his hat aside, removed his gunbelt, and sank down to join her there.

As she poured their drinks, Ollie sighed and said, "I'll just never understand you boys. Why do you act so silly about us girls? Why can't you just come out with what you want from us instead of shooting one another over poor lonesome widows who don't even know they might be wanted?"

Longarm sipped at his wine. It was a tad weak, but refreshing. He said, "To begin with, us boys learn early on that you girls tend to scream as if you've seen a mouse, should a mere male even hint he'd like to invite you to swim naked on such a warm afternoon."

She arched a brow and demurely asked, "Oh? Did I just hear somebody hinting?"

Longarm laughed sheepishly and said, "By way of illustration, Miss Ollie. You were supposed to scream and climb up on a chair. I told you I had a train to catch."

"What if you missed it?" Ollie asked, rolling on to her knees to unbutton her bodice as she added, "What if we went . . . swimming and you caught a later train in, say, a month or so?"

He had to tell her a month was out of the question, even as she shucked her habit to show she'd been wearing nothing under it, and damned if he hadn't been right about long underwear having way too much to hide. But as she rose in all her naked glory, like Miss Venus from her seashell in that painting, he had to allow he could catch a train come Monday with nobody in Denver being any the wiser.

So she laughed and dove gracefully into her private swimming hole, to be followed by Longarm as soon as he could shuck his infernal boots and duds.

The water felt just right, and they enjoyed the first few laps together until, naturally, they wound up in the shallows more like mating frogs than playful sunfish.

So as sassy Polly Eastman peeked at them on her belly in the sage, she had to laugh. For Aunt Olivia and her new boyfriend weren't doing it at all like horses did it, albeit they seemed to be having a lot of fun.

Watch for
LONGARM ON A WITCH-HUNT

279th novel in the exciting LONGARM series
from Jove

*Coming in February!*

**Explore the exciting Old West with one of the men who made it wild!**